6/15 NEB X

RUTHLESS

ALSO BY JOHN RECTOR

RUTHLESS

JOHN RECTOR

THOMAS & MERCER

Published by Thomas & Mercer, Seattle.

www.apub.com

Amazon, the Amazon logo, and Thomas & Mercer are trademarks of Amazon.com Inc. or its affiliates.

ISBN-13: 9781477827628
ISBN-10: 1477827625

Cover design by David Drummond

Library of Congress Control Number: 2014957294

Printed in the United States of America.

For Zoe

PART I

I had time to kill, so I stepped into Mickey's Pub to get out of the rain. It was a nice enough place, clean and warm with a dark cherrywood bar, and a long cut-glass mirror that reflected the soft amber light of the room.

Mickey stood behind the bar. He had a paperback in his hand and thick-rimmed reading glasses sitting low on the bridge of his nose. When he saw me, he closed the book and set a rocks glass on the bar in front of me.

"Didn't expect to see you tonight," he said, reaching for the Macallan bottle on the shelf behind him. "Big plans this evening?"

"Just waiting out the rain."

Mickey took off his glasses and folded them into his breast pocket. Then he uncapped the bottle and filled my glass. "Never seems to stop, does it?"

"No," I said. "It never does."

Mickey put the bottle back on the shelf, and I sipped my drink, silent. I could hear the whisper of a radio somewhere in the back room, Bob Dylan singing "Forever Young" in the distance. I thought about that as I drank.

"How's your old man doing these days?" Mickey asked. "Feeling any better?"

"About how you'd expect."

"That's too bad. He's a good man."

I nodded, but I didn't say anything.

Behind me, the door opened and several men wearing off-the-rack suits came in, loud and wet from the rain. They stopped just inside the door, looked around, then muttered to themselves and walked out.

"I was thinking about you the other night," Mickey said. "My wife's brother is putting a game together this weekend. I thought you might want a seat."

"Your brother-in-law?"

"And his asshole broker friends," he said. "They're looking for an excuse to get away from their wives and kids so they can get drunk and—"

"Lose their money?"

Mickey smiled. "They'll figure that part out later."

"What's your cut?"

"Twenty percent. Thirty if we do it together."

"Have you been practicing?"

"I'm getting there."

I set the glass in front of me and ran my finger along the rim. "I take it you don't think much of your brother-in-law."

Mickey leaned in close. "Tell you the truth, I can't stand the son of a bitch, but my wife's been on my ass to be nice to the guy, so . . ." He turned and grabbed a bottle from the top shelf and two shot glasses from the counter. "What can I do? He's family."

He set the shot glasses between us and filled them both. "What do you think? Want to make some easy money?"

I'd been around long enough to know that there was no such thing as easy money. Still, hearing the excitement in his voice made me smile. He was right about one thing: the game did sound promising—and I was broke.

"What's the buy-in?"

"A grand."

"Jesus."

"Don't worry about that," he said. "I'll front you, help you build a new bankroll."

"Bad idea," I said. "With the way my luck's been running, I'm not a good investment."

He waved me off.

"These guys are fish, Nick. Even if you're off your game you'll still walk out with more than the buy-in." Mickey tapped the bar with his finger. "You could be out of the hole after one night."

"It'd have to be a hell of a night."

"One for the ages, my friend." He held his shot glass up, waited for me. "What do you say?"

"Let me think about it."

Mickey's eye twitched, and his smile faded. "You need to think about it?"

"It's been a long time," I said. "Things didn't end well for me."

"I'll need to know by Friday."

"That's fair."

Mickey watched me for a moment longer. Then he reached out and touched his glass to mine, and we both drank.

It burned in the best possible way.

I set the shot glass upside down on the bar. "Wow."

Mickey was quiet, and when I looked up at him I noticed he was staring past me toward the front of the room. I turned and saw a woman in a black raincoat standing just inside the door. She was alone, shaking the rain from a half-closed umbrella and staring at me.

I turned back to the bar.

Mickey winked at me and walked away.

———

"Are you him?"

The woman stood a few steps behind me. She was older than me, blonde, and polished to a shine. There was a large designer purse over her shoulder, and she held it tight against her body. I'd never seen her before, but the way she looked at me gave me hope.

I decided to play along.

"That depends," I said. "Are you her?"

The woman exhaled and glanced back toward the door. Her body seemed to relax and grow tense at the same time, and for a second I thought she was going to walk out, but she didn't. Instead, she set her purse on the bar and slid out of her coat.

The move looked practiced, as if for effect.

It was a good effect.

"You're early." She draped her coat over one of the bar stools and sat next to me. "I was hoping to have a drink before you showed up."

Her voice was slurred, and the smell of alcohol rolled off her in waves. It was obvious that I had some catching up to do.

"Sorry," I said. "I didn't know."

"We said eight o'clock." She looked at her watch. It was a gold Rolex. "It's a quarter till."

"I've never been good with time."

Her eyes narrowed.

"A joke." I shook my head, motioned to Mickey. "Forget it. What are you drinking?"

"Vodka martini."

I repeated the order to Mickey. He nodded and took a martini glass from the back shelf, set it on the bar, and then reached for the vodka. When he finished the drink he speared an olive with a plastic sword, dropped it in the glass, and set it in front of her.

"How about you?" Mickey said. "Ready for another?"

I nodded and pushed my glass across the bar toward him. He refilled it and pushed it back.

The blonde was quiet until Mickey was gone, then took the speared olive out of her drink and tapped it on the rim of her glass.

"I'm not entirely sure how this works," she said. "I've never done anything like this. I'm a little nervous."

"It's easy," I said. "All you have to do is lift your glass and drink."

The blonde stared at me. "Another joke?"

"Apparently not."

This time I thought I saw the hint of a smile.

"You're cute," the woman said. "I didn't know what to expect when I came here, but it certainly wasn't a sense of humor."

"Are you disappointed?"

"Intrigued more than anything." She lifted the speared olive to her mouth, pulled it away with her teeth, chewed. "I don't meet men like you every day."

"Men like me?"

The woman nodded, then took a paper napkin from the stack on the bar and touched it to the corner of her mouth. "I'm a little out of my element."

"Don't worry," I said. "I'll be gentle."

She laughed, soft but genuine.

"I may be out of my element, but I'm far from delicate."

"Then I take it back."

"Are you saying you won't be gentle?"

I felt a low buzz at the base of my spine, and I smiled at her. She smiled back.

Part of me knew the game had gone on long enough and that I'd taken it too far. Eventually, she was going to realize her mistake and leave, embarrassed. I knew that drawing it out was a shitty thing to do, but it'd been a long time since I'd shared a drink with a beautiful woman, and I didn't want it to end just yet.

"Tell me," I said. "What were you expecting?"

"Does that matter?"

"I'm curious."

The woman took a deep breath, then turned and leaned in, studying me. Up close her eyes were dark, and the skin around them was puffed red, as if she'd been crying.

I stared back, waiting for her to answer.

A moment later the softness in her eyes faded, and she pulled away.

"What I was expecting isn't important," she said. "All that matters is that I can trust you."

"Trust me?" I made a dismissive noise and took a drink. "Oh, you can trust me. Just ask around."

"Believe me, I have."

There was something in her voice that I didn't like, and for the first time since she sat down a warning light flashed bright in the back of my mind.

I ignored it.

The woman lifted her drink and finished it. She set the empty glass on the bar and reached for her purse. I thought she'd finally had enough of me and had decided to leave, but then she opened her purse and took out a thick manila envelope.

I watched her, not looking away.

She held the envelope in her lap, staring at it as if trying to decide. Then she set it on the bar and slid it over to me.

"What is this?"

"Everything you wanted." She stood and shouldered her purse. "It's all in there, including half the money. You'll get the rest when she's gone."

The words seemed to hang in the air.

"You have one week." The woman took her raincoat from the stool and started for the door. "Not a day longer."

"Wait," I said. "What are you . . . ?"

My voice cracked, and the woman kept walking.

I looked down at the envelope and tried to tell myself that I hadn't heard her right. Either that or this was some kind of joke.

Except I had heard her right, and it wasn't a joke.

A small voice in the back of my mind whispered through the noise, telling me that there was still time. I thought if I hurried I could catch her, but when I turned, all I saw was the door closing behind her as she walked out into the rain.

I grabbed the envelope and flipped it over and fumbled with the metal clasp on the back, feeling the weight of the situation settle around me.

I opened the envelope.

There was a banded stack of hundred-dollar bills inside, along with a silver flash drive and a photograph of a young woman in a yellow dress standing on a white pier overlooking the sea.

I took the photo out and held it in front of me.

The small voice in the back of my mind was still talking to me, telling me that I needed to do something to fix this before it was too late.

Except this time it wasn't a whisper.

It was a scream.

I dropped the photo back into the envelope and headed for the door. When I stepped outside, the rain slapped cold against my face, sobering me. There were people everywhere, huddled under umbrellas and moving in a steady wave along the sidewalk.

I stood in the rain, scanning the crowd as the seemingly endless flow of bodies pushed past.

I didn't see the woman anywhere.

2

"How'd it go?"

I sat back on the stool and reached for my glass. I finished what was left of my drink, then set the envelope on the bar and tried to think about what I needed to do next.

"Not good, I take it."

I looked up at Mickey. "What?"

"The blonde." He pointed toward the door. "I saw the way she ran out of here. I'm guessing it didn't go the way you expected."

"No," I said. "It didn't."

Mickey laughed under his breath. "Don't let it get you down, Nick. When you lose one there's always another waiting on deck."

Mickey kept talking, but I barely heard a word of what he was saying. I was still trying to make sense of what'd just happened, but I couldn't do it.

I flipped the envelope over, opened the flap, then took out the photograph and held it up in the dim light. The girl in the yellow dress was beautiful and several years younger than me. Her skin was smooth and tanned, and her hair was sun-streaked blonde. There were no worry lines on her face—at least not yet—and her eyes looked clear and happy.

And yet someone wanted her dead.

I turned the photo over.

There was an address written in black ink on the back. I made a mental note of it, then slipped the photo back into the envelope and took out the flash drive. There were no markings on the surface, and no hint of what might be on it.

All that was left was the money, but I didn't touch that. If I had to guess, and if all the bills in the stack were hundreds, then I figured there was at least ten thousand dollars inside. I wouldn't know for sure unless I counted it, but Mickey's wasn't the place for that.

Also, I wasn't sure I wanted to know.

What I needed to do was call the police and explain what had happened, but I'd been around enough cops in my life to know exactly how that would go. While I didn't like the idea of spending the rest of my night answering questions, I didn't see any other choice.

It was the right thing to do.

I sat for a while longer, finishing my drink and letting the idea of calling the police sink in. Then I opened the envelope and dropped the flash drive inside.

This time, curiosity got the best of me.

I reached in and flipped through the stack of bills. They were all hundreds, and there were a lot more than I'd originally thought.

I can pay Kara back.

The idea came to me all at once, and when it hit, it hit hard. I tried to tell myself that it wasn't my money to spend, but it was too late. The idea dug into my brain like a tick, making it impossible to ignore.

"Ready for another?"

I looked up and saw Mickey holding the bottle over my glass, waiting.

"No, I'm done." I set the envelope on the bar. "What do I owe you?"

Mickey replaced the bottle on the shelf. "Tonight or total?"

"Total."

He told me.

I looked down at the envelope for a long time, then I reached in my pocket and took out my checkbook. I flipped to a blank and started filling it in.

"Do me a favor and don't cash this for a few days."

Mickey nodded, silent.

I tore the check out and handed it to him. He looked it over, then tried to hand it back.

"You can get me later," he said. "After the game, when it won't sting so much."

"I never said I'd play, only that I'd think about it."

"We both know you'll play." He set my check on the bar and pushed it across to me. "But either way, don't worry about this today. I know you're good for it."

"Take it anyway. It's yours."

Mickey shook his head, walked away.

I left the check sitting on the bar, and I didn't say anything else about it. Then I picked up the envelope, closed the flap, and fastened the metal clasp on the back.

"Can I use your phone? I left mine at home."

"If you want privacy, use the pay phone up front."

The walk from the bar to the pay phone seemed long, and the envelope felt heavy in my hand. I knew calling the police was the right thing to do, and usually that would be enough, but this time something was different. This time the answer wasn't as clear.

When I was a kid, my father told me that sometimes opportunities came in unexpected places, and that a smart man knew how to spot them and take advantage.

Except I'd never been a smart man.

By the time I got to the pay phone, the idea of keeping the money was all I could think about. All I had to do was keep walking. The blonde didn't know my name or who I was, and there was no way she'd be able to find me again.

Just open the door and walk away.

I almost went through with it, but then I thought about the girl in the yellow dress. If I walked away, the blonde would most likely try again, except next time she'd show up sober and she'd get it right. That would make the girl's death as much my fault as hers.

I knew it was true.

The girl was in danger, and I was the only one who could help her, but I still stood by the pay phone for a long time, trying to decide. It wasn't until the door opened into me and a man came in from out of the rain that I snapped out of it.

The man was wearing a dark raincoat with a hood. When he saw me, he pulled the hood back and smiled, flashing a single gold tooth.

"Sorry, pal. Didn't see you there."

I told him it was fine and stepped out of the way, letting him slip past me into the bar.

Once the door closed behind him, I reached for the phone and dropped some change into the slot. The number for the police was printed on the front of the phone, but I didn't need it. I still knew the number by heart.

I dialed and listened to it ring.

As I waited, I watched Mickey through the small window in the door. He took my empty glass and set it in the sink behind the bar. Then he picked up my check and ran a white towel over the spot where I'd been sitting.

He set the check back on the bar.

I shook my head. "Stubborn motherfuc—"

On the phone a woman answered. "Police."

I turned away from the window and pressed the receiver against my ear. "Can I speak with a detective, please?"

"Is this an emergency?"

"No, but it's important."

"What's it regarding?"

"I'm not sure," I said. "I guess . . ."

I glanced back toward the bar and saw the man with the gold tooth taking off his coat and setting it on one of the bar stools. He was wearing a blue button-up shirt with the sleeves rolled up to his elbows. The skin on his arms was covered in an intricate tapestry of ink.

He sat at the end of the bar, hands folded together in front of him, waiting.

I felt a small knot of panic form in my chest.

"Sir?"

"Yes."

"What is this regarding?"

I watched through the window as Mickey approached the man in the blue shirt, and I could see his lips moving around his smile. Then the man said something, and Mickey stopped talking.

All at once I heard the blonde's voice in my head. It was only two words, but they were enough.

You're early.

"Sir?"

I snapped back. "Yeah, sorry."

"I need to know what this is regarding." The woman on the phone sounded tired and impatient. "It's the only way I can get you to the right department."

"I understand," I said. "How about homicide?"

I heard the rapid click of fingers on a keyboard, then the woman said, "Hold, please," and the line went silent.

I looked back toward the bar.

The man in the blue shirt was still talking, while Mickey listened and nodded. I started to wonder if I was being paranoid, but then Mickey lifted his head and glanced at me over the man's shoulder.

It was a quick look, but it was enough.

The man turned and followed Mickey's gaze. For a second our eyes met, and neither of us looked away.

"Homicide, Detective Reed."

The man in the blue shirt stood up.

The voice on the phone said, "Anyone there?"

"Sorry," I said. "I made a mistake."

I hung up as the man in the blue shirt started walking back toward the door. He never took his eyes off me.

I stepped back, squeezed the envelope tight, and then pushed the door open and ran outside.

The rain was coming down hard, and it soaked through my shirt, chilling my skin. I cut through the traffic on the sidewalk and ducked under a moving canopy of umbrellas, following the flow of the crowd.

My first thought was that I needed to get home, where I could regroup and figure out a plan, but when I turned onto Sixteenth Street I saw a blue and white city bus slow to a stop halfway down the block.

I ran toward it, weaving through the crowd.

I was a few steps away when the doors hissed shut.

"Shit."

I slammed my hand against the door as the bus started to pull away from the curb. The driver looked down at me, frowned. Then he stopped and opened the door.

"Next time wait for the next one."

I thanked him, then looked back over my shoulder as I climbed on. I didn't see the man anywhere, but I wasn't ready to believe that I'd lost him—not yet.

I paid the fare and sat in the first open seat.

As the bus pulled away, I stared out the window, watching for the man in the blue shirt. At first I didn't see him. Then the crowd parted, and he was there, standing on the corner, scanning the street through a silver sheet of rain.

Then the bus turned, and he was gone.

3

I rode the bus to the end of the line, then got off and looked around for a phone. The terminal was dark and nearly deserted. The only people I saw were huddled in corners or asleep on the scarred wooden benches lining the walls.

An old man in a white City Transit shirt was pushing a broom across the linoleum floor. He saw me and nodded.

I asked him where I could find a phone.

The old man stopped sweeping and leaned against his broom. He studied me without making eye contact, then waved a hand in the direction of the ticket window.

"You got pay phones that way," he said. "If you can find one that works. Don't you have a cell phone?"

"Forgot it at home."

The old man shook his head and went back to sweeping.

Before he turned away, I noticed several deep red gin blossoms blooming along the man's nose and cheeks. Under the terminal's harsh fluorescent lights, they looked dark and almost alive, like a scattering of spiders.

I followed his directions to a line of pay phones next to the ticket window. I picked the first one I came to, then fished some change from my pocket and dialed.

The phone rang three times before Mickey answered.

"Mickey's."

"Hey, it's Nick."

For a moment the line was quiet.

"Are you there?" I asked.

"Jesus, Nick. What the hell did you get yourself into?"

It was a good question, but I didn't have an answer.

"What did he say?"

"Before or after you ran out of here?"

"Both," I said. "I need to know everything."

"He wanted to know about the blonde. I told him she came and went and that he should ask you, since you were the one who talked to her." He paused. "I wasn't thinking. I'm sorry."

"Did he come back after I left?"

"Grabbed his coat," Mickey said. "What's this all about? Was that her husband?"

"Did he say anything when he came back?"

"Not much, I—"

"Anything at all," I said. "It's important."

Mickey was quiet for a minute, and I could tell he was choosing his words carefully.

"He asked who you were. I told him your first name when he mentioned the blonde, but I didn't give him any more than that."

I closed my eyes and leaned against the wall by the phone. The tension in my shoulders and chest was starting to fade, and for the first time I allowed myself to think that everything was going to be okay. He'd seen my face, but he didn't know who I was or where to find me. He could look, but tracking me down was going to be nearly impossible.

"Do me a favor," I said. "Let me know if he comes back or if anyone else shows up asking about me."

"What the hell is going on, Nick?"

"I can't talk about it now. Just let me know if anyone starts asking about me."

"Yeah, of course."

I looked at my watch. "I've got to go, but I'll call again later."

"Nick?" Mickey hesitated. "How bad is this? How much trouble are you in?"

"I'm not sure yet."

"Can I help?"

Across the terminal, a woman lying on one of the benches stood up and started screaming and kicking the wall, telling it not to push her around. No one else seemed to notice.

"I'm going to go home and lie low for a while," I said. "Wait for this to blow over."

Mickey was quiet, and I didn't like it.

"What is it?"

"I don't think you should go home."

"Why not?"

Mickey exhaled into the phone. "He saw your check."

At first I didn't know what he was talking about, but then it came to me, and I felt my stomach twist. The check—we'd argued over it, and I left it sitting on the bar.

"What do you mean he saw it?"

"He took it."

"My name's on that check," I said. "My address."

"When he came back, he asked about you, then grabbed his coat. I thought he was going to leave, and I wasn't paying attention. I only noticed your check was gone after he left."

"Did he know it was mine?"

Mickey didn't say anything.

"Tell me you didn't tell him."

"No, not a word."

"But he knew."

"Yeah," Mickey said. "He knew."

———

After I hung up with Mickey, I sat on one of the wood benches and tried to figure out my next move. I couldn't go home—at least not yet—and I needed a place to stay.

There was only one option.

I checked the bus schedule and took the number 19 to the Southside and got off a few blocks from my father's place.

Capitol Liquors was across the street from the stop. I went inside and picked up a six-pack and a bottle of Knob Creek.

My father was easier to handle if you brought gifts.

As I left the liquor store, I thought about what I was going to say when I got to his house. He was going to know something was wrong, and I wanted to have it all straight in my head before I saw him, but the more I thought about it, the more mixed up I felt.

All I knew was that I couldn't go home until I had an idea of how much danger I was in. The man in the blue shirt had seen my face, and since he had my check he also knew my name and address. All I had were the rain-soaked clothes I was wearing and a stack of hundred-dollar bills that would probably end up getting me killed.

At least the rain had stopped.

—————

My father still lived in the house where I grew up. He bought it when I was a kid, a couple years before my mother died. In all that time I'd never heard him talk about moving. Even after the neighborhood started falling apart around us he went along as if nothing had changed.

That stubbornness was his strength.

Despite everything that'd happened, he kept us together and grounded. We'd had hard years, but through them all he was always there.

When I got to his house, I walked up the steps to the porch and knocked on the door. It felt weird to knock, but he wasn't expecting me, and he was usually armed.

I adjusted the bag from the liquor store in my arms and waited. I didn't hear anything inside, so I knocked again. This time there were footsteps. They stopped on the other side of the door and then there was nothing.

I was about to knock again when I heard a woman's voice say, "Who is it?"

"It's Nick."

I listened as she slid the chain free and turned the bolt locks. When she pulled the door open, I smiled.

"Hey, Penny."

"Hello, Nick." She pushed the screen door open and stepped to the side. "You know you don't have to knock around here. This is still your home."

It was nice of her to say, but she was wrong. This place wasn't my home and it hadn't been for a long time, but I didn't say that to her.

"I didn't know you were here today," I said. "And I didn't feel like getting shot."

Penny leaned her head back and laughed. The sound was full and genuine, and it made me smile despite it all.

"You're a wise man, Nick. Very wise indeed."

Penny had been my father's nurse for the past year. She used to come once a week to check in on him, but over the past couple months she'd been coming every few days. Soon she would come every day, and eventually she'd move into my old room and stay for good, but that was something we didn't talk about.

"What brings you all the way out here?"

"Came by to visit," I said. "How's he doing?"

"Still a shithead." Penny looked from me to the bag then back, frowning. "What's in the bag?"

If I'd known she was going to be there, I would've planned ahead, but I didn't and now I was caught.

"You're not going to take it away, are you?"

Penny stared at me, still frowning, but I could tell it was a struggle.

"I'll pretend I didn't see anything, but just this once." She held up a finger. "I was on my way out anyway, so let's just say I missed you."

"That would've been too bad," I said. "You know I don't come here to see him."

"A young man's flattery." Penny looked at me sideways and grabbed her purse off the table by the door. "You could teach him a thing or two." She put a hand on my arm and leaned toward the hallway and my father's office. "I'm leaving, Charlie." No answer. "And your son is here, so don't shoot him."

I heard a loud cough, then my father's voice. "Can't promise anything."

Penny patted my arm and started for the door. I held it open for her as she walked out onto the porch.

"It's always nice to see you, Nick," Penny said. "You should come by more often."

"You're right," I said. "I'll try."

I offered to walk her to her car, but she refused, so I stood at the door and watched her until she was out of sight. Once she was gone, I carried the bag to the kitchen. I took two glasses from the cabinet and pulled the bottle from the bag. Then I set the manila envelope on the counter and stared at it for a while, debating whether or not to show it to him right away.

In the end I decided to wait.

4

I poured a drink and handed it to my father. He took the oxygen tube from his nose, sipped the drink, and eased back in
his recliner. He didn't say anything, but I knew the look, and I
could tell he was happy.

"You're not torturing Penny, are you?" I asked. "If you
chase her off, you're on your own. Your pension won't cover
another nurse."

He waved a hand in the air, dismissing the thought, then
pointed to the small television sitting on a tin TV tray against
the wall. The game was on, and the camera panned over the
home crowd, filling the screen orange.

"Every year it's the same goddamn thing," he said. "They
hit the play-offs and they choke. It's unbelievable."

"But you keep watching."

"Of course I do. That's the deal."

I didn't say anything else, and for a long time we sat in silence as the announcers droned on and the crowd roared through a broken three-inch speaker.

When he finished his drink, he held the glass out.

I poured him another.

"Are you going to tell me what's going on?"

"As soon as I figure out where to start."

"How much trouble are you in this time?"

"Hard to tell," I said. "Maybe none."

"But maybe a lot?"

"Yeah," I said. "Maybe a lot."

Charlie sipped his drink, then set it on the end table next to his chair and coughed for a long time. When he stopped, he reattached his oxygen and sat with his eyes closed until the wheezing faded and his breath returned, cycling in and out, slow and steady.

I considered asking him if he was okay, but I knew better. Instead, I set my glass on the floor by my chair and said, "I have something to show you."

I walked out to the kitchen and grabbed the manila envelope off the counter and brought it to him. He took it, turned it over in his hands, and looked up at me, waiting for an explanation.

"I met a blonde in a bar," I said. "She—"

"You met a blonde in a bar?" He laughed. "Any story that starts like that isn't going to end well."

I ignored him and kept going.

"She thought I was someone else, and I let her go on thinking it." I nodded toward the envelope. "She gave me that before she left."

Charlie straightened the metal clasp on the back. "What do you mean, she thought you were someone else?"

"She was there to meet someone and she thought I was him." I reached for my glass on the floor. "She was drunk, and I played along."

"Why the hell would you do that?"

"I thought it would be fun."

He shook his head, then opened the flap and looked inside. His expression didn't change.

"She told me that was half and that I'd get the rest when the job was done."

"Those were her exact words?"

"She said, 'When she's gone.'"

My father reached into the envelope, and I could tell that he was counting. When he finished, he closed the flap, set the envelope on his lap, and reached for his drink.

"There's twenty grand in here."

I didn't say anything.

"Who's the young lady in the photo?"

"No idea," I said. "There's an address on the back, but no name."

"Why didn't you call it in?"

"I started to, but then he showed up, so I left."

Charlie's eyes narrowed. "Who showed up?"

"The guy the blonde was there to meet," I said. "And that's the problem."

———

Charlie listened as I went over everything that'd happened, and to his credit he didn't insult me once.

I think that worried me more than anything.

By the time I finished, it was dark outside. Another storm had moved in, and the soft rattle of rain against the side of the house made me think of Kara and better days.

"Mickey was right. You shouldn't go home."

"I'll have to eventually."

"Not tonight," he said. "Stay here. We'll figure out something else in the morning."

"Do you still have friends down at the station?" I asked. "I want to know more about that girl."

"Why?"

"To warn her," I said. "I want to help her if I can."

Charlie looked at me with a strange mix of humor and pity. "What do you think you're going to do, sweep in and save her, like she's some princess trapped in a tower?"

I didn't answer.

Charlie shook his head. "How this shit happens to you, I'll never be able to figure. I swear, Nick, you are a magnet for trouble."

"Is there someone down there who can help or not?"

"I've got a few guys who owe me favors," he said. "But this is dangerous territory. You should've turned this over to them the second you figured out what was going on."

"I told you, I—"

"Yeah, I know." Charlie raised a hand, stopping me. "I get it. You tried. Your intentions were good, but something went wrong. Sorry if I've heard it before."

I inhaled deeply, held it, counted, said, "It's not too late. I can still tell the police. Let them handle it."

"That won't solve your problem," he said. "If this guy knows where you live, telling the police isn't going to help you."

"Isn't that their job description?" I asked. "You helped people."

"Things have changed since I was a cop." He leaned forward and pushed himself up to his feet. "These days the job is more about punishing than protecting."

"You don't really believe that."

"I believe what I see." He dropped the envelope on my lap. "You hand that over to them now and all they'll do is take it away and send you home. They won't get involved unless there's a body. You know how it works."

He was right, I did.

"Okay, so no cops."

"Not unless you want to give them the money and hope the guy it was meant for doesn't come looking for it."

"What do you suggest?"

I watched him consider his answer, and for a moment I was struck by how different he looked than the man I knew when I was a kid. Back then he'd been a giant, and his shadow fell over every part of my life. Now he was smaller, his arms thinner, his back bent. The disease had changed nearly everything about him—everything except his eyes.

His eyes were exactly the same.

There were a few more lines around the edges, but the color was still solid and so dark that it was hard to see where the iris ended and the pupil began.

When I was a kid, he told me his eyes looked that way because he was part shark. I believed him, too.

It explained a lot.

"I think I'm going to sleep on it." Charlie grabbed the handle of his oxygen tank and rolled it toward the hallway leading back to his bedroom. "I've never trusted my first instinct."

"But you have an opinion."

"Of course I do."

"Then tell me."

He stopped in the doorway. "You won't like it."

"I don't like any of this."

Charlie raised a hand to his mouth and coughed. "I think you should leave town. Get out of here for a while. Wait for all of this to blow over, then come back."

"And go where?"

"Wherever you want." He pointed to the envelope. "You've got the money. Pick a place."

"And what about the girl?" I held up the envelope. "She should know what's going on."

"How will that help her?"

I stared at him, silent.

"You're not seeing this situation clearly, Nick."

"It seems clear enough to me."

A deep line formed between my father's eyebrows. For a moment I thought he was going to argue, but instead he turned away and started down the hall toward his bedroom.

"Stay here tonight," he said. "We'll talk again in the morning."

"It'll be the same conversation."

"We'll see." He didn't look back. "You'll have to clear the boxes off your bed. Go ahead and stack them on the floor. Clean sheets are in the closet."

I watched him drift down the hall until he faded into the shadows, then reached for my drink and finished what was left in the glass. I flipped the envelope over on my lap, took out the photo of the girl in the yellow dress, and stared at it for a long time. I studied her face and the slow curve of her dress and tried to imagine what she could've done to make someone want her dead.

Outside, the rain fell soft against the window.

I closed my eyes and listened.

5

The next morning I woke to the smell of fresh coffee and the sound of coughing. I pushed the sheets back and sat on the edge of my old twin bed and tried to shake the morning haze out of my head. When I felt ready, I pushed myself up, got dressed, and walked out into the kitchen.

Charlie was sitting at the breakfast table. There was an old TV on the counter, but the sound was turned down, and he wasn't watching. He had a cup of black coffee and an open newspaper in front of him, and an unfiltered cigarette burning between his fingers.

"Penny would kill you if she saw you smoking."

"I doubt it." He flipped the paper over, refolded it. "She's got a thing for lost causes."

"Lucky for you." I took a coffee cup from the cabinet, filled it, and then sat across from him. "Do you want some breakfast?"

He shook his head and pushed the section of the paper he'd already read across the table to me. I unfolded it and sipped my coffee as we fell back into a forgotten routine.

When I finished my part of the paper, I dropped it on the table and leaned back in my chair and said, "Did you have an epiphany overnight?"

Charlie took a long drag off his cigarette, then crushed it in a glass ashtray on the table. When he spoke, he didn't look up from his paper.

"Do you remember my friend Lonny down in Tucson?"

"What about him?"

"I talked to him this morning," he said. "About you."

"Why?"

"He owes me a favor, and I thought he could help out with your situation."

"What did you tell him?"

"Nothing specific." He grabbed his cup and drank the last of his coffee, then got up and walked to the counter for a refill. "He's got a fishing cabin down in Mexico. I told him you needed to get out of town for a while, and he said you could stay there if you don't mind doing a few repairs on the place."

"Mexico?"

"You'll have to meet him in Arizona to get the keys, but after that—"

"I'm not going to Mexico, Pop."

Charlie leaned back against the counter, holding his coffee cup with both hands. "It's not forever."

"My life is here. I can't just leave."

"Of course you can."

"And just run away?"

"No one is telling you to run, only to be smart." He motioned toward the kitchen window. "This guy out there, do you know who he is or what he's capable of doing? Do you know anything about him at all?"

"I don't even know that he's looking for me," I said. "Their deal was a bust. He's probably long gone by now."

Charlie stared at me without saying a word. He didn't have to. I knew exactly what he was thinking.

"You think I'm being naive."

"I think someone is out twenty grand," he said. "They know you took it, and they know where you live. It's stupid to think they're going to walk away and let you keep it."

I lifted my cup and swallowed the last of my coffee. "Maybe, but I can't leave."

"Because of Kara?"

"Because of Kara. Because of you." I paused. "Because of the girl in the photo—all of it."

"A girl you've never met and who you know nothing about."

"Does that matter?" I asked. "Someone wants to kill her. I have to try and help her."

"How do you plan on doing that?" Charlie walked around the table to his chair and sat. "Do you think you can just go up to her, introduce yourself, and then casually mention that someone hired you to kill her? How do you think that's going to go over?"

"I'll deal with that when I have to," I said. "But it would be easier if I knew something about her first."

"And what about Kara?"

"What about her?"

"Take her with you."

"To Mexico?" I laughed. "That'll never happen."

"You don't know until you ask," he said. "Talk to her, apologize for being you, and then tell her you want to take her on a long trip. Call it a new beginning."

"Like it's that easy."

"Why not?"

I shook my head, looked away.

On TV the news was on, showing the weather report for the rest of the week.

There was only rain.

"Do you know what your problem is, Nick?"

"Here we go."

"You've seen too many goddamn movies. And it's not just you. Everyone today thinks love has to be something magical and unique that sets them apart from the billions of other people in the world."

"That's not what I'm—"

"Love is the simplest thing in the world. You find someone who thinks like you and then make a commitment." He tapped a finger in the air between us. "Whatever problems you two have, Kara thinks like you."

"Not about everything."

"She does about most things." He braced his arms on the table and leaned closer. "Do you want to know the secret to making a marriage last?"

He didn't wait for me to answer.

"You don't get divorced."

"That's it?"

"There's no other way to do it, and anyone who tries to tell you differently is full of shit."

"I don't think it's that simple, Pop."

Charlie sat back and sipped his coffee. "That's because you've seen too many movies."

I didn't have anything else to say, and we both sat there, quiet. I thought about Mexico and the possibility of taking Kara with me. After a while, it didn't seem all that impossible, at least not from my side.

"Kara won't go to Mexico," I said. "She doesn't trust me."

"She might if you tell her the truth."

The idea of telling Kara what'd happened at Mickey's made my chest ache. It'd taken a while just to get her to talk to me again, and we still had a long way to go before things were back to the way they were. I didn't want to take a step back, not over this.

"You're not going to say anything to her, are you?"

"Not if I don't have to."

Charlie shook his head. "Jesus, Nick. You never learn."

"What about you?" I asked. "You'll be here alone."

"Me?" Charlie laughed, and the laugh turned into a cough. When it passed, he smiled, said, "I'll be fine without you. The girl comes every few days."

"The girl's name is Penny."

He waved the name away, pointed at me. "If you're using me as an excuse to stay and get killed, stop that shit right now. I'll still be here when you get back."

"I never said you wouldn't be."

"Yeah, but the thought crossed your mind."

He was right, it had.

The emphysema was in the early stages. He could still get around and only had to use his oxygen when it got bad. Unless something else happened, he'd be here in a year when I came home. And he was right about Penny. She was a good nurse, and she took good care of him. More importantly, she could handle his moods. If he gave her a hard time, she'd take it with a smile and then give it right back.

"Mexico is a long way to go," I said. "Especially if this turns out to be nothing."

"And what if it's not nothing?" he asked. "I've seen normal, everyday people do batshit crazy things for a lot less money than what's in that envelope."

I let that sink in, and for a while neither of us spoke. As much as I hated the idea of leaving, part of me couldn't help but see the logic in it.

And then there was Kara.

Thinking about taking her along had touched something inside of me that I thought I'd buried a long time ago. I even let myself imagine what it would be like, the two of us together again, sitting side by side on a sun-soaked beach, staring out across white sands toward an endless crystal-blue sea.

It was a tough image to shake.

"What about the girl in the photo?" I asked.

Charlie studied me for a moment, frowned. "I'll make you a deal. I'll see what I can find out about her for you, but then you head south."

"After I tell her what's going on."

"If that's what you want," he said. "Do we have a deal?"

"We have a deal."

Charlie smiled, then pushed away from the table and crossed the room to the counter. He opened the top drawer and took out a familiar black key chain. He set it on the table in front of me before sitting back down.

"What are you doing?"

"You're going to take the car," he said. "I've got it running nice. It'll get you to Mexico and back, no problem."

I didn't know what to say. The car—my father's car—was a black-on-black 1966 Chevelle SS396. He'd picked it up at auction several years ago and had been restoring it ever since. The car was his obsession.

"I'm not taking your car."

"You'd rather ride the bus to Mexico?" He paused, smiled. "Look, Nick, I'll help you find out about this girl, but I need to know you're safe. I'd feel better knowing you had a decent car."

I looked down at the keys on the table, then reached out and picked them up. What he said made sense, but I'd never heard him talk like this before, and I wasn't sure what to say.

In the end, I just nodded and said, "Thanks, Pop."

He grinned at me.

"What?"

"Come on," he said. "Let's take a look at her."

I smiled and got up from the table. As I turned away, something in the paper caught my eye. I stopped and picked up the page.

The photograph was of a man and a woman standing together behind a glass podium, surrounded by the press. The man had his hand on the woman's back, while she held a large pair of gold scissors over a long red ribbon. There was a banner behind them, strung between two cement posts.

It read: "Holloway Industries."

I stared at the photo for a long time.

Charlie waited. "You coming?"

"That's her," I said. "Right there."

He stepped closer. "Who?"

I studied the photo for a moment longer, wanting to be absolutely sure. Then I handed him the page and tapped my finger against the photograph.

"That's the woman who gave me the envelope."

6

We walked out the back and down a stone path lined with dead rosebushes toward the detached garage. Charlie opened the side door and we went inside. There were two windows on either wall, both coated with years of grease and dust, and the light shining through was warm and easy, the color of new pennies.

The car was covered by a stained canvas tarp.

Charlie took one corner and said, "Help me with this."

I took the opposite corner and pulled.

My breath caught in my throat.

I hadn't seen the car since he dragged it home from the auction. At the time it wasn't much more than a rusted shell. I knew he'd put a lot of work into it after he'd retired, but I wasn't prepared for what I saw. The car was sleek and spotless and polished to an angry black shine. I reached out and touched the fender. The metal felt warm under my fingertips, and for the first time in my life I thought I understood his obsession.

"Are you sure about this?" I asked.

Charlie put his hand on my shoulder, squeezed, then pulled away just as fast. "As long as you bring it home safe."

I nodded, didn't say anything.

Charlie moved to the front of the garage and opened the overhead door while I went around to the driver's side and slid in behind the wheel. The leather seat moaned under me as I turned the key in the ignition and felt the engine rumble to life. The sound was low and heavy, and it vibrated through to the center of my chest. I sat back, adjusted the mirror, and then put it in gear and backed out into the alley.

Charlie came around to the driver's side and leaned in. "Give me a call this afternoon," he said. "I'll let you know what I find out about the girl."

I told him I would, but before I could say anything else, he turned, tapped the roof with his hand, and walked back into the garage. He stopped just inside and pulled the overhead door closed.

Charlie had never been one for good-byes.

————

Traffic heading into downtown was light, and it didn't take long to get back to my neighborhood. When I pulled off the highway, I drove past Mickey's, then turned onto Tenth and headed south toward my apartment. I drove slow, scanning the street for anything that looked out of place.

Nothing did.

I parked a block away and walked up the alley to my apartment. If someone was watching my building and waiting for me to show up, I figured they'd most likely watch the front door. I didn't know if that was true or not, but it made me feel better.

The alley behind my building was empty. As I got close, I fished my keys out of my pocket and flipped through them until I found the right one. Then I unlocked the back door and went inside.

The rear stairwell was dark and the air smelled wet and sour, like rotting wood. The blue and green carpet on the stairs was worn to thread in the middle, revealing the scarred floors underneath. There was a single lightbulb mounted on the wall, but the shadows in the stairwell were thick, and the light didn't cut through.

Once I got to the third floor, I opened the door enough to look out. From where I stood I could see my apartment and the long, empty hallway leading toward the elevators at the front of the building. I walked quickly to my apartment, unlocked the door, and went inside, sliding the bolt lock behind me.

I set the manila envelope and my keys on the table, then went through the apartment, checking all the rooms and closets. When I was sure that I was alone and everything was the way I'd left it, I went back to the living room and grabbed my cell phone from the coffee table and called Mickey's.

A girl, whose voice I didn't recognize, picked up after the third ring. There was a lot of noise in the background, and she yelled into the phone. "Mickey's."

"Is Mickey around?"

She told me she'd check. A couple minutes passed, then Mickey picked up. I told him who it was. Then I heard someone in the background shout and laugh.

Mickey sighed, said, "For Christ's sake, hold on a minute."

He put the phone down and said something to someone off the line. A moment later another line picked up and Mickey said, "Okay, got it."

There was a click, and the background noise was gone.

"Nick?"

"You sound busy."

"Some insurance convention over at the Hilton. They picked this place to get away from it."

"Champagne troubles?"

"Depends on how you look at it," he said. "I take it that blonde's husband never tracked you down."

"He wasn't her . . ." I caught myself before I said anything else. As much as I wanted to tell Mickey the truth, I figured the less he knew, the safer he'd be.

"Has he been back?" I asked.

"Not while I've been around," Mickey said. "Sounds to me like you dodged a bullet."

We both laughed, even though I didn't find it funny.

"Have you thought about the game this weekend?" he asked. "I need to know if you're in."

"I'm not," I said. "I've got to leave town for a while."

"How long?"

"Not sure." I walked across the living room and into the kitchen. "A while."

"Like a week?"

"Longer than that." There was a dirty plate in the sink and two empty paper cups on the counter. I dropped the cups in the trash, then took a beer from the refrigerator. "Closer to a year."

"You're kidding?"

I told him I wasn't.

Mickey hesitated. "You're not telling me something."

I walked back to the living room and grabbed the manila envelope off the table. Then I sat on the couch and took a long drink, choosing my words carefully.

"Something came up," I said. "It's a new start and a good opportunity."

Mickey exhaled into the phone. "Damn, and I was looking forward to seeing the look on my dipshit brother-in-law's face when we took all his money."

I smiled. "Next time."

Mickey and I talked for a while longer. I told him I'd stop by to settle my tab before I left town, but I didn't know if I'd be able to keep that promise. I hoped I could. I liked Mickey. He was one of the few people I'd miss when I was gone.

After I hung up, I leaned back on the couch and put my feet up on the coffee table. It was nice to be home, and I sat there for a while just enjoying the feeling.

It'd taken a long time to get used to living alone. Kara and I had been together for nine years, and when we split up the adjustment had been more difficult than I'd expected. It took a while before I appreciated having a place all to myself, and now I was leaving it behind.

I finished my beer, then went back into the kitchen for another. I didn't know how long it would take before Charlie heard back from his contact at the police station, but I figured I had a few hours to kill, plenty of time to finish off the last of the beer in my refrigerator.

I opened two and carried them out to the living room. When I got to the couch, I set the bottles on the coffee table, then took the flash drive out of the envelope.

I turned it over in my hand.

Eventually, curiosity got the better of me. I grabbed my laptop, turned it on, and plugged the drive into the side. When I clicked on the icon it prompted me for a passkey.

I frowned, drank the rest of my beer, and then closed the laptop. I pulled the flash drive and dropped it back in the envelope, then started working on the second beer.

I stayed on the couch for a while, looking around my apartment and thinking about what'd happened over the past couple days. I didn't want to leave, not without Kara, but also because this was my home. When I finished my second beer, I got up and headed to the kitchen for another.

As I passed the bookshelves, something caught my eye, and I stopped.

There was a check sitting on the top shelf. It was propped against a framed photo of Kara that I'd taken on our honeymoon, and as I reached out to pick it up, everything inside me fell away.

Even without reading it, I knew.

It was the check I'd left for Mickey.

7

I dialed Kara's number and listened to it ring while I went through my apartment again, searching all the rooms for anything else I might've missed the first time. After the fifth ring, it rolled over to voice mail.

"Shit."

I hung up and dialed again. This time Kara answered.

"What do you want, Nick?"

There was an edge to her voice, and it surprised me, but it didn't stop me. She was home and she was safe.

"Is everything okay?" I asked.

Kara paused. "Why wouldn't it be?"

"When you didn't answer, I thought maybe—"

"I didn't answer on purpose," she said. "But I knew you'd keep calling until I did."

"I was worried about you."

"Worried about me?" Kara laughed. "Come on, Nick."

"I don't know why you're angry, but I didn't call to—"

"You know exactly why I'm angry."

I stopped talking.

"Answer one question for me," Kara said. "Can you do that?"

"I'll try."

"What gives you the right to check up on me?"

"Don't you think you're overreacting?"

"Answer the question."

I frowned. "I was worried about you, Kara. I had a bad feeling, and I wanted to hear your voice, that's all."

"Why couldn't it wait until today?"

"What are you talking about?"

"I'm talking about last night," she said. "You know I'm working two jobs right now. What were you thinking calling me in the middle of the night?"

I opened my mouth, but there were no words.

"You can't do that, Nick. It's not okay."

I felt a small knot of fear form in my chest, and I swallowed hard against it. "What time last night?"

"Don't do that."

"Kara, I didn't call you last night."

She sighed. "Your name came up on my phone. I know it was you. Please don't lie to me."

I took the phone away from my ear and checked my call history. Kara's number was at the top. Two calls just past 3:00 a.m.

The knot in my chest grew.

"Are you even listening to me?"

"I'm listening." I put the phone back to my ear and tried to think. "I don't know what to say."

"Did you think I had someone over? Was that it?"

"No," I said. "I—"

"Because that is none of your business. We aren't together anymore. I can do what I want."

"I know," I said. "I'm sorry."

Kara was quiet for a moment. When she spoke again, the edge in her voice was gone, replaced by a tired sadness.

"Don't do it again, Nick. We've been getting along lately, and it's been nice. We're not seventeen anymore, so don't act like it."

As she spoke, I walked back to the bedroom and took an old gym bag from my closet. I unzipped the top and started shoving clothes inside. I thought about telling her the truth about what'd happened, but I didn't want to drag her into it if I didn't have to. She'd put up with enough from me over the years, and I didn't want to add anything new to the list.

"I'd like to talk to you," I said. "It's important."

"Talk about what?"

"About us," I said. "Our future."

Kara exhaled into the phone. "I'm not in the mood right now. I didn't sleep last night, and—"

"I have to leave town for a while."

Silence.

I kept talking. "I don't know how long I'll be gone, but I'm leaving tonight."

"You're kidding, right?" Her voice sounded thin and empty. "Do I even want to know why?"

"One of Charlie's friends has a place in Mexico. He's looking for someone to stay down there and do a few repairs."

"Why you?"

"Because I can do the job," I said. "And a change of scenery might be nice."

"You're not exactly the lie-on-the-beach type."

"Maybe not," I said. "But I want to try, and I want you to come with me."

Kara was quiet.

"Are you there?"

"Yeah, I'm here."

"It could be a new start for us," I said. "This place is right on the ocean, and it'll be just the two of us."

"Are you in trouble?"

"Kara . . ."

"Do you owe someone money?"

"No," I said. "Nothing like that."

"Then what is this?"

"I thought if we went away together, just the two of us, that we could fix things."

"You're serious?"

"Yes, I'm serious." I shoved the last of my clothes in the bag and set it by the door, then reached under my bed and pulled out my gun safe. "I want us to start over."

Kara hesitated. "No, Nick."

"Why not?"

"You're asking me to pack up and leave everything in my life behind after you've proven that you can't be trusted." She paused. "Of course I won't go with you."

I sat on the edge of the bed, silent.

I'd prepared myself for her to say no, but I wasn't ready for the finality of her answer or for how sure she sounded about the decision. Hearing her say no hit harder than I'd expected, and it stung.

"I thought we were getting better."

"We are, but . . ." She paused. "Nick, there are some things we need to talk about."

"So talk."

"Not now," she said. "I'll come by your place tomorrow."

"I'm leaving tonight," I said. "I'll come over there and we can—"

"No, Nick."

I stopped talking. "You don't feel anything for me anymore?"

"You know that's not true."

"Then I don't get it," I said. "Why not try again? We can make it work this time."

"I have my reasons."

"You don't trust me?"

"Should I?"

I wanted to say yes, but I couldn't.

"What can I do?"

"Tell me the real reason you're leaving town."

"I told you, Charlie has a friend who needs someone—"

"Not that bullshit story. Tell me the truth."

"That is the truth."

Kara sighed. "Good-bye, Nick."

"Wait—"

"Tell me the reason you're leaving, or this conversation is over."

"Kara, wait a second, I—"

"Last chance."

Again, I thought about telling her everything, and this time I almost did, but then I thought about the check I'd found sitting next to her photograph and I changed my mind. It could've been random, but I didn't think so. He'd chosen that spot because he'd wanted to send a message, and it'd worked.

Until I had a better idea about what was going on, I couldn't risk telling her the truth.

"If you come with me, I'll tell you everything."

"Jesus, I knew it." She laughed. "Is this really the life you want?"

"What do you mean?"

"You were happy at the paper," she said. "You had a career. What happened?"

"The Internet," I said. "Sign of the times."

"Blame the world if you want, but you never even tried to find another job. You gave up and you decided to play cards instead."

"We needed the money."

"No." Her voice was sharp. "You do not get to blame this on us. Everything you did was your choice. You made your own decisions."

"I wanted to take care of you."

"I never needed you to take care of me."

"That's not what I meant."

"Then explain it."

I tried to keep my thoughts straight, but the conversation was spiraling away from me, and I didn't know how to stop it.

I decided to be honest.

"I still love you," I said. "And I want you back."

"For how long?" she asked. "How long until you disappear again? How long until I get a call saying you're in jail, or in the hospital because someone caught one of your moves and beat you half to death?" Her voice cracked, and when she spoke next there were tears behind her words. "I can't do that again, Nick. I won't."

"You'll never have to."

"You say that, but—"

"Let me prove it to you."

"It's too late, Nick."

"Come with me," I said. "I've been waiting for the right time, and this is it. This is our chance."

Kara didn't say anything for a long time.

Then she did.

"I'm sorry," she said. "You waited too long."

The line clicked, and she was gone.

I sat on the edge of my bed with the phone pressed against my ear, listening to the silence. I stayed there for a while, letting her words sink in. Then I hung up and looked down at my watch.

It was getting late.

I got up and opened the top drawer of my dresser and took out my passport and a small silver key. I slipped the passport into my pocket, then knelt next to my gun safe and slid the silver key into the lock and turned.

The lock clicked, and I opened the lid.

The case was empty.

My gun was gone.

8

It was time to leave.

I went out the back door into the alley and across the street to where I'd parked. There were more people around than when I got there, and I kept my head down as I walked and tried to not make eye contact. Once I got to the car, I put my bag in the trunk, climbed in behind the wheel, and started the engine.

My hands were shaking, and I squeezed them into fists to make them stop. It didn't work, so I closed my eyes and tried to force myself to relax. Usually, taking a minute to stop and breathe helped calm my mind, but not this time.

Everything had changed.

The man I saw at Mickey's had not only seen my face, he'd been in my apartment. He knew about Kara, and now he had my gun. To make things worse, I couldn't report it stolen without telling the cops about the blonde and the money, and that wasn't an option. I'd waited too long and there would be too many questions.

That meant it was time to go.

I opened the glove compartment and shoved the manila envelope inside. Then I put the car in gear and pulled out onto the road. I'd only gone a few miles when I noticed a black SUV three cars back, matching my speed. I switched lanes and made a few extra turns, watching the SUV in my mirror the entire time.

Every move I made, they matched, always three cars back.

"Shit."

The highway was coming up, and I was about to turn onto the on-ramp and really see what the car could do when my phone rang. I picked it up and checked the ID: Charlie White.

I answered. "Hey, Pop."

"How's the car?"

I glanced back at the SUV in my mirror and said, "Runs good, but the paint scratches too damn easily."

"Aren't you fucking hilarious." He tried to sound mad, but I could hear the smile in his voice. "I thought I'd let you know that I heard back about that girl in the photo. Still interested?"

After discovering someone had been in my apartment and that they'd stolen my gun, tracking down the girl from the photo seemed like an unnecessary risk. Still, I'd asked Charlie for a favor, and he'd come through for me. There was no harm in hearing what he found.

"Why not." I drove past the highway, then changed lanes. The SUV moved with me. "But I've been thinking about what you said, and maybe you're right. Maybe I should get out while I can."

"What changed your mind?"

"What good is it going to do?" I asked. "She'll either think I'm crazy or that I'm dangerous."

"Did something happen?"

"You mean on top of everything else?"

Charlie hesitated. "What's going on, Nick? You were set on this a few hours ago. Why the change of heart?"

He already knew the situation, and I was about to tell him what I'd found in my apartment, but then he started coughing and I didn't get the chance. I glanced back at the SUV and listened to my father cough and struggle for breath. This time, something in me changed. The fear was gone and all I felt was anger.

I pulled to the side of the road and hit the brakes.

At first I thought the SUV was going to pull in behind me, but when it got close I heard the engine rev, then watched it speed past. I tried to get a look at the driver as he went by, but all I saw was a shadow.

I stayed there until the SUV disappeared down the road. Then I pulled back out into traffic.

On the phone, Charlie stopped coughing.

"You okay?"

"My lungs are rotting away but other than that I'm fine." He coughed again, louder this time, and when he spoke next, his voice was strained and choked. "You want to hear what I found out or not?"

"Depends," I said. "Anything good?"

"I'll let you decide." He shuffled through papers, then said, "The girl's name is Abigail Pierce. The address on the back of the photo is hers. It's a nice place, too, just off Jefferson Park."

"She owns it?"

"No," he said. "The name on the deed is Daniel Holloway, her father. I didn't find anything on employment for her, so I'm guessing she doesn't pay rent on the place."

"Then she has money."

"I don't know about her, but her father does. Quite a lot, actually."

"Holloway," I said. "From the paper this morning?"

"That's right," Charlie said. "Daniel Holloway owns Holloway Industries. They have labs and a research and development facility on the west side, along with shipping warehouses in Carson City. As far as I can tell, they work mostly with academia, but they also have a couple good-sized government contracts."

"Sounds big."

"You can say that," he said. "As it turns out, Daniel Holloway is one of the richest men in the state."

"That still doesn't tell me anything."

"Here's where it gets interesting." Charlie cleared his throat, and when he spoke he sounded ten years younger. "I didn't find too much on the girl, Abigail. She's twenty, no criminal record, no real employment history. We're tracking down her medical records. They should come back in a day or two.

We know she landed in the foster care system as a teenager, but she ran out in the first year. Beyond that, nothing."

"So, that's it?"

"Basically, she's a good kid with a clean record."

"Then I don't get it," I said. "Why would someone want her dead?"

"That's why I decided to look into her family," Charlie said. "The majority of these types of cases end up leading back home, so it seemed like a good place to start. I had my contact check on her father first."

"And?"

"Daniel Holloway had a stroke a few weeks back, a bad one. He spent a significant amount of time in intensive care over at Penrose Hospital, and he was recently released against doctor's orders. His wife took him home."

"I'm still not seeing your point."

"His wife is Patricia Holloway."

I stopped talking. "The woman in the newspaper."

"That's right," he said. "She's your blonde."

I thought I should say something, but there were no words. In the end, all I managed was "Holy shit."

Charlie laughed. "So there you have it."

"The blonde is Abigail's mother?"

"Stepmother most likely," Charlie said. "She married Daniel fifteen years ago."

I stopped at a red light and leaned back in my seat, letting this new information sink in.

"Why would she want her dead?"

"Who the hell knows why people do what they do?" Charlie said. "In most of these cases it usually comes down to love or money. We know the girl's dad is loaded, and from the sound of it he's not long for this world."

"You think this is about money?"

"No idea, but I bet the answer is in his will."

"Christ," I said. "What a family."

Charlie was quiet for a moment. I heard the quick scrape of a cigarette lighter, and then he was back, exhaling long and slow into the phone.

I kept my mouth shut.

"I think you're doing the right thing, Nick. Your intentions are good, but this isn't something you want to get involved in. It's better to let it sort itself out."

I listened, but my mind kept drifting back to the girl in the photo. I thought about her smile and the way the sunlight touched her skin. Then I thought about the blonde sitting next to me in the bar, the smell of alcohol on her breath, her eyes swollen and red.

None of it made sense.

Up ahead the light turned green, and the car behind me honked. The sound brought me back, and I sat up and pulled out into the intersection.

Charlie was still talking, but I cut him off.

"Listen, Pop, I've got to go."

He stopped.

"It's a lot to take in."

"All right," he said. "But do me a favor and think things through before you make any decisions. You got it?"

"Yeah," I said. "I got it."

"Let me know if you have any problems in Tucson."

I told him I would, and then I hung up.

I drove back toward the highway, then headed south toward Tucson. I did my best to stay focused on the road ahead, but all I could think about was the girl in the yellow dress, happy and shining in the sunlight.

The road hummed beneath me.

I drove for a long time before I turned around.

9

Jefferson Park used to be a cemetery.

It'd been excavated after World War II to make room for the city's growing population, and it hadn't changed much since. The houses were brick, the sidewalks were stone, and the streets were quiet and lined with rows of towering oak trees.

It was 1950s perfect.

Still, as I drove along the wide, shaded streets, I couldn't shake the feeling that I was making a mistake. Finding the girl in the photo seemed like the right thing to do, but it was also careless, especially after everything that'd happened.

If I were smart, I'd be long gone.

The address was easy to find, but I didn't stop. Instead, I drove by and circled the block. I still had no idea what I was going to say to her, and I had no idea how she would react when I told her. It was possible that my good intentions were about to land me in jail.

I made a long pass around the park, then cursed myself for wasting time. If I was going to talk to her, then I needed to do it and get it over with.

I drove back to the house and parked a block away next to a long wall of lilac bushes. The bushes were tall, and they shielded the car from the house. That way, if she did decide to call the police, I could leave without her seeing me. It wasn't the best escape plan, but it was better than nothing.

I opened the glove compartment and reached for the manila envelope. I held it in my lap long enough to change my mind about taking it along. I wanted this to look like a casual visit, but if I showed up carrying the envelope she'd know something was wrong.

I put the envelope back, then got out and locked the door. The bad feeling was still there, but it was quieter now.

I took that as a good sign.

From the outside, Abigail Pierce's house looked small. It was one level, brick, with a bay window facing out toward the street. The front door was painted red, and there was a weathered metal door knocker hung in the center, just below eye level.

It was shaped like a turtle.

I reached for the door knocker, then changed my mind and rang the bell.

The house was silent.

The only sounds I heard were the wind in the trees and the thin rumble of a lawn mower in the distance. I walked to the edge of the porch and looked in the front window. I held my hand against the glass to block the glare, but it didn't help much. All I could see was a coffee table, a red couch, and a large red and black painting hanging on the wall.

No one was home.

I felt a warm buzz at the thought, but I ignored it and told myself I couldn't leave, at least not yet.

I went back to the door and rang the bell again.

This time when no one answered, a wave of relief rolled through me. There was a comforting voice in my head telling me I'd done what I could. I'd tried to warn her, but it didn't work out, and now it was time to go.

I didn't argue.

Then I heard a voice behind me.

"Use the knocker."

I looked back and saw an old man in gray slacks and a Rolling Stones T-shirt standing on the sidewalk. He was holding a leather leash attached to a tiny brown poodle.

"What?"

"She's probably got her headphones on," the old man said. He pushed his glasses up on his nose, then motioned toward the door. "Use the knocker. She'll answer."

"Thanks, but it looks pretty quiet. I'll just come back some other time."

"She's in there," he said. "She's always in there."

I stood, not moving.

The excitement I felt a moment ago was still strong, but it was fading fast. I turned back and reached for the turtle and knocked three times. The sound was loud, and it echoed through the neighborhood. If the old man was right and she was home, there was no way she wouldn't hear it.

"Are you a friend of hers?" the old man asked.

"Not exactly," I said. "I know her father."

"Do you now?" The poodle at the man's feet sniffed the ground, squatted. "Abby doesn't talk much about her family. How is it you know—?"

I heard a bolt lock slide, and I turned around just as the door opened. Abigail Pierce stood in the doorway. She looked at me for a moment, her face young and bright and open, and when she smiled it shone in her eyes.

"Abigail?" I asked.

"Do I know you?"

I opened my mouth to speak, but the old man on the sidewalk interrupted.

"He's a friend of your father's," he said. "He was about to leave, but then I told him to use the knocker. Did you have your headphones on?"

Abigail gave me a knowing grin, then looked past me to the old man. "I did, thank you, Glenn."

"Anytime, sweetheart." He raised one hand, waved, and then said something to the poodle that I didn't catch. He pulled the leash tight, and before he walked away he nodded at me and said, "Nice meeting you, friend."

Once he was gone, I turned back to Abigail. She was wearing an oversized black T-shirt and loose-fitting black sweatpants. Her hair was pulled back in a ponytail and held in place with a pink hair tie. She looked so much like the photo that for a moment all I could do was stare.

"So . . ." She let the word hang in the air. "How do you know Daniel?"

The question snapped me back. "What?"

"My father?" She pointed past me toward the sidewalk. "Glenn said you two know each other."

"Right," I said. "Actually, I know him. He wouldn't have the slightest idea about me."

"I see." She leaned against the doorframe, arms crossed over her chest. "So you're one of those."

"One of those?"

"A Holloway disciple," she said. "You people read all of his papers and follow him around like he's some kind of messiah. Isn't that your thing?"

"Not my thing."

She studied me, frowned. "Maybe not. You don't exactly fit the type."

"What type is that?"

"The type that looks like they masturbate to the periodic table."

I wasn't sure what to say to that, and for a moment we just stood there, staring at each other. Then I laughed, held out my hand.

"Nick White," I said. "It's nice to meet you."

"Abigail Pierce." She took my hand. "Abby."

Her skin felt soft against mine, but her grip was strong and confident. I couldn't help but like her.

"Are you here to talk to me about Daniel, or is there something else?"

"Maybe both," I said. "Can I come in?"

Abby looked at me hard, and I could tell she was trying to decide if I was a threat. She must've figured I wasn't, because she stepped back from the door and motioned me inside.

"Have a seat." She led me to the red couch. "Do you want a drink? I have water."

"No, thanks."

"There's also vodka and scotch, or I might have beer in the refrigerator."

"Okay," I said. "Scotch."

Abby disappeared through a doorway into the kitchen. I heard a cabinet open, then the refrigerator, followed by the bright clink of ice in glasses.

"If you're not one of Daniel's followers," she said from the kitchen, "then how do you know him?"

"To tell you the truth, I've never actually met him."

The sounds in the kitchen stopped and for a while there was only silence. When Abby reappeared in the doorway, she was carrying two half-filled glasses. She handed one to me, then sat on the other end of the couch.

"You're not going to make me regret inviting you in, are you, Nick?"

"I hope not."

She stared at me, then sipped her drink and said, "Maybe you should tell me what you want."

"You're right," I said. "I'm sorry."

I swirled the scotch in my glass, then lifted it and downed it all. The burn hit the back of my throat and spread through my sinuses, warming me all the way through. When I reached out to set the glass on the coffee table, I noticed Abby smiling at me.

"You good?" she asked.

I cleared my throat, nodded.

Abby laughed, lifted her drink, and finished it in two swallows. She set the empty glass on the table next to mine, then eased herself into the corner of the couch, resting her elbow on the back cushion.

"Now we're even," she said. "So why don't you tell me why you're here?"

I didn't know if it was the scotch or if it was the way she was looking at me, but the nervousness I'd felt before was fading. She deserved to know what'd happened, and I wanted to tell her everything. How she took the news wasn't important.

All that mattered was the truth.

Once I started to talk I couldn't stop.

10

Abby came back from the kitchen with new drinks, and this time the glasses were full. She held one out to me, and I noticed her hands were shaking.

"Sorry for all this," I said. "I thought you had a right to know."

She sat on the couch, staring at nothing, and took a drink. "I'm glad you told me."

"If it were me, I would've wanted to know."

She looked up at me. "When are you leaving town?"

"Tonight," I said. "First Tucson and then on to Mexico. I figure the sooner I'm on the road, the better."

"The woman who approached you," she said. "Are you sure it was Patricia? Are you positive?"

I told her I was, then added, "She'd been drinking quite a bit before she approached me."

"That sounds like Patricia," Abby said. "She considers herself to be an expert on how other people should behave, but those rules rarely apply to her."

Abby looked down at her glass, silent.

I tried to imagine how I'd react if a total stranger showed up at my door and gave me the same news I'd just given her. I wasn't sure I'd be as calm, but people dealt with stress in different ways. Still, Abigail Pierce didn't seem concerned. If anything, she seemed at peace.

"Are you okay?" I asked.

Abby looked up, lost in thought. "What?"

"You don't seem surprised by any of this," I said. "Are you going to be all right?"

"Honestly, I'm not sure," she said. "How are you supposed to act in these kinds of situations?"

"I wish I knew," I said. "I think if I found out that someone in my family had tried to hire someone to kill me—"

"My family?" Abby laughed, quick and harsh. "That woman is not my family."

I stopped talking. Abby must've seen the look on my face because when she spoke next, there was pity in her voice.

"Do you mean this entire time you thought Patricia Holloway was family?"

"But Daniel Holloway is—"

"My father." She nodded. "And Patricia Holloway is his wife, but that's all she is. I certainly don't think of her as a mother. My mother's been dead for almost six years."

"I didn't know," I said. "I'm sorry."

Abby shrugged. "It's been a long time."

"You must've been young."

"I've never been that young." She set her glass on the coffee table, then adjusted herself on the couch, tucking one leg under her. "Did someone tell you that Patricia was my mother?"

"No, I just—"

"God, I can't imagine." She laughed. "What a nightmare—for both of us."

"I take it you two don't get along."

Abby's eyes narrowed. "You came here to tell me that she hired you to kill me."

"Right." I held up a hand, waving away the question. "I'm a little mixed up. Part of me was expecting you to think I was crazy, but you don't seem shocked at all."

"I hide it well," she said. "Truth is, I'm terrified. That woman is insane."

"But you're not surprised?"

"No, not surprised." Abby leaned over, picked up her glass, and took a drink. "Patricia has hated me since the first time I spoke to Daniel. The only thing that surprises me about any of this is that she waited this long."

She looked down at her glass, spun the ice.

"After the paternity test came back showing that I was his daughter, she hated me even more." Abby looked up at me and tried to smile. "Funny, isn't it? I've never done anything to that woman except exist."

"There was a paternity test?"

"Patricia insisted on one," she said. "I agreed to it, of course. Daniel wanted it, too. He's a sweet man, but he's not an idiot. When you're worth that kind of money, you don't just open your arms and your checkbook to every stray kid that steps in off the street claiming to be yours."

"But you are his daughter?"

"No doubt about it."

I eased back on the couch, laughed under my breath. "Were your mother and Daniel married, or did they—?"

"Married?" Abby shook her head. "God, no. My mother was a waitress. She met him in between wives."

"How long were they together?"

"I don't know all the details," she said. "She didn't talk much about him. I think it went on for a while, and eventually it just faded out."

"Did you see him when you were growing up?"

"Never."

I heard a clock chime in one of the other rooms. I turned and looked out the bay window. The sun was starting to go down, and the shadows along the street were long and fading.

"It's getting dark."

Abby turned toward the window, but I could tell she wasn't really seeing.

"I used to think about him when I was a kid," she said. "I'd wonder where he was and if he ever thought about me. I never did find out."

"Your mother didn't stay in contact with him?"

She shook her head. "I decided to track him down after she died. All I had to go on was an old photo and a faded business card. It wasn't much, but it was a trail I could follow. When I finally found him and told him who I was, he was a little surprised."

"I bet."

"I was worried that he'd be angry, but he wasn't. The first time he saw me, he squeezed me so tight I could barely breathe. It was wonderful." Abby stopped talking, ran her fingertips under her eyes. "Such a sweet man."

"Makes you wonder why he married Patricia."

"Patricia wasn't his first wife," Abby said. "That one drowned off the coast of Martha's Vineyard forty years ago. Patricia came into the picture after Daniel's split with my mother. They don't get along. I'm not sure they ever did."

"And then you showed up."

"It was bad before me," Abby said. "And the last few years have been a nightmare. If she hadn't been so horrible to him, he might not have had this stroke."

"That's terrible."

"She's terrible," Abby said. "She has two kids from a previous marriage, and she thought marrying Daniel would set them up for life. Then I came around, and all of that fell apart for her."

I listened, letting the pieces fall into place.

Before, I couldn't imagine why Patricia would want Abigail dead. Now, after hearing her story, it all started to make sense.

"I think the will was the last straw for her," Abby said. "He told her he'd provide for her and her kids but that he was leaving the bulk of his estate to me, and that I would be his primary beneficiary."

"That had to have been hard to hear."

"She had everything figured out, but thanks to me it's all gone." Abigail paused. "The money doesn't even mean much to me. It sounds dumb, but I'd rather have him."

I thought about that for a moment, then said, "What would happen if you die before he does?"

Abby tried to smile. "I guess that would change things, wouldn't it?"

Neither of us said anything, and for a long time we sat quietly on the couch as the sun went down and the air outside turned from gold to blue. Things were coming into focus, but the more I learned, the more I realized that there was nothing I could do to help her.

Abby turned to me. "Can I ask you something?"

"Of course."

"How much did she offer to pay you?"

"There was twenty grand in the envelope," I said. "She told me it was half and that I'd get the rest once you were gone."

"Forty thousand dollars?" Her eyes went wide. "That's a lot of money."

"Yes, it is."

Abby leaned back on the couch, sinking deeper into the cushions, and laughed. "I guess I should feel flattered."

I looked over at her, didn't speak.

Eventually, she stopped laughing and began to cry.

11

I opened the door and walked out onto the porch. The street was dark and quiet, and the moon hung low and bright over the trees. Abby followed me, stopping just outside the door, and leaned against the house.

"Listen," I said. "If you want to go to the police, I'll go with you."

"They'll never believe us." Abby tried to smile. "I barely believe any of this myself."

"We've got the money. That'll at least get their attention."

"We still don't have enough proof." She stopped talking and looked up at me, her eyes wet from tears. "Part of me is happy that you got her money. It serves her right."

I thought that was an odd thing to say, but I didn't press. Instead, I stood there until the silence turned uncomfortable, then asked, "What are you going to do?"

Abby looked down at her feet, shook her head. "Move, I guess. Find someplace they'll never look for me and start over." She glanced up at me. "Ever been to Nebraska?"

"I'm not even sure I could find it on a map."

Abby smiled, but there was no humor in it.

"Sounds perfect."

I glanced over my shoulder at the street, then turned back to her. "Is there anything I can do?"

"You can take me with you to Mexico," she said. "I'm little. I won't take up much space."

I didn't know what to say to that, and when I opened my mouth to speak I stumbled over my words.

Abby laughed and held up her hand, stopping me. "I'm kidding," she said. "I'll be fine."

I took my wallet out of my pocket. "Here, let me—"

"I don't need money, Nick."

"It's a phone number, just in case."

"A phone number?"

"My father," I said. "He used to be a cop. He might be able to help if something happens."

I dug through my wallet, but then Abby stepped forward and put her hand over mine.

"Thank you," she said. "But I'll be okay."

"Are you sure?"

Abby looked up at me and frowned. "Why are you doing all of this? Why did you come here tonight?"

"I felt like I owed it to you."

"You don't even know me."

I shrugged. "It seemed like the right thing to do."

She stared at me, and I could see the amusement behind her eyes. "Most people wouldn't see it that way." She paused. "You're an interesting man, Nick."

Before I left, Abby leaned in and gave me a hug and told me to be safe. And as I walked down the path toward the street, I thought about what she'd said.

You're an interesting man, Nick.

I didn't see it.

———

Halfway to the car, the wind picked up and the leaves in the trees rattled around me like a chorus of insects. I turned and looked back toward Abby's house, but I'd gone too far, and all I saw was the golden glow of the streetlights lining an empty road.

Something wasn't right.

Part of me had hoped I'd feel relieved after talking to her. I thought it would be like a weight lifted, making the decision to keep the money and leave town that much easier to stomach. Instead, it felt like a mistake. All I'd done was deliver bad news to a scared young woman. I showed her that the family she'd hoped to find after her mother died hated her and wanted her dead.

I showed her that she was alone.

I thought about her situation as I walked the rest of the way to the car, and I had to remind myself that while Abigail

Pierce was young, she wasn't a child, and she could take care of herself. She'd already survived the death of one parent and had managed to track down her birth father on her own.

She was tougher than she looked, and that gave me hope.

When I got to the car, I took the keys from my pocket and unlocked the door. I was about to get in when I noticed a man standing alone, halfway down the street, hidden in the shadows between the streetlights, watching me.

I stood there, staring at him, but he didn't move.

I told myself I was being jumpy and that he was probably just a neighbor out for a walk, nothing more. I almost believed it, too, but then the man raised a hand to his mouth and a dull red glow lit his face.

His eyes were focused on me.

The urge to get in the car and drive away was strong, but I pushed it back. I took the key and walked around to the back of the car. Then I opened the trunk and dug around until I found the tire iron.

I'd never used a weapon on anyone in my life, and I didn't know what I planned on doing with one now. All I knew was that I liked the feel of it in my hand, and if the man standing on the street was out there for me, I wanted to face him with more than words.

I closed the trunk and walked out into the street, but when I looked at the spot where the man had been standing, he was gone.

I stood there, scanning the shadows, and tried to ignore the growing feeling that I was being watched.

This time when the urge to leave hit, I went back to the driver's side of the car and climbed in. As I started to pull away from the curb, something in the rearview mirror caught my eye.

There was a black SUV parked half a block away.

I turned in my seat and looked out the back window, squinting against the darkness. I tried to believe that it was a coincidence. I even told myself that there were hundreds of black SUVs on the road and that this wasn't the same one that had followed me that afternoon.

I wanted to believe it, but I didn't.

I felt the tension build in my chest, and I squeezed the steering wheel tight. I knew if I ran they'd follow me, and this time they might even catch me. But as I sat there, listening to the low rumble of the engine, I couldn't help but like my chances.

I was about to drive away when another thought struck me, knocking all the air out of my lungs.

They're not here for me.

It took a moment for this to sink in, but once it did, I knew it was true. Of course they weren't here for me. They wanted Abby. And I'd led them right to her.

A low ache started in my chest, and I realized I was holding my breath. I let it out slow, then looked down at the tire iron on the passenger seat.

Maybe it wasn't too late.

I grabbed the tire iron and got out. The SUV was dark, and I couldn't tell if anyone was inside or not.

I ran back to Abby's house. I thought if I hurried I could get her out and take her someplace safe. I didn't know where, but that didn't matter as long as it was away from here.

When I got to her house, I ran up the path to the porch. The lights were still on inside, but the blinds were closed. I reached out to knock, but before I could the door opened.

The man standing in the doorway was wearing the same blue shirt I'd seen him in the day before. Everything about him looked the same, except this time he was holding a gun, and it was pointed at my stomach.

"Hello, Nick."

I looked past him and saw Abby in the hallway. There was another man with her. He had one hand over her mouth and was pinning her arms behind her with the other.

Abby's eyes were wide and terrified.

"Come in," the man in the doorway said. "Let's talk."

I heard something move behind me, and I turned around.

The man I'd seen on the street was coming up the path toward the house. When he got to the porch, he took his cigarette from his mouth and flicked it into the grass, then reached down and took the tire iron from my hand.

I turned back to the man in the blue shirt. "You don't have to do this."

The man smiled at me, and a single gold tooth winked under the porch light.

He didn't say a word.

12

The man in the blue shirt motioned me inside.

"My name is Victor. The man behind you is my brother, David." He thumbed back over his shoulder. "The gentleman behind me is Mr. Ellis."

"What do you want?"

"We'll get to that," he said. "Right now I need you to put your hands behind your back."

Next to me, David took a plastic zip tie from his pocket and formed it into a loop.

I stepped to the side. "Wait a minute, I—"

"Nick?" Victor still had the gun aimed at my stomach, and his voice was slow and calm. "I'd very much like for this conversation to be a friendly one, but that's up to you. It certainly doesn't have to be."

I could feel myself start to panic, and his words barely made it through the buzz in my head. All I knew was that I couldn't let them tie my hands. I couldn't lose control.

David moved closer, reached for my wrists.

"Wait." I pulled away. "I can give the money back. There's no reason—"

"We'll talk about that," Victor said. "But first I need you to—"

"No." I backed up, and the adrenaline buzzed through me. "I'm not going to let you—"

David stepped in behind me.

I felt his hand on my shoulder, and as I pulled away there was a violent pain at the base of my spine. I heard a rapid popping sound that seemed to hang in the air, and then all the strength ran out of my legs. I dropped to my knees and hit the floor facedown, my muscles twitching.

I heard Abby scream, but the sound was far off and muted. David knelt down and pressed his knee into the back of my neck and pulled up on my arms. He fastened the zip tie around my wrists, and the plastic dug into my skin. When he finished, he grabbed my shoulder and rolled me over onto my back. Victor slipped the gun into the back of his belt, then knelt down next to me. They each took an arm and lifted me to my feet.

The air had a peppery, burnt-hair smell that settled in the back of my throat and made it hard to breathe. I swallowed hard and fought the urge to be sick.

Victor and David moved me to the couch and helped me sit. I leaned forward and closed my eyes and waited for the spinning to stop and the world to refocus.

Victor was saying something to David that I couldn't hear. When he finished, David nodded and walked out of the living room. He returned a minute later with a black kitchen chair and set it across from me.

Victor took the gun from his belt and sat on the chair. He studied me for a moment, then said, "How are you feeling?"

I didn't say anything.

"I do apologize for this." He motioned to my hands with the gun. "The thing is, I can get a little jittery. It's better for us all if I don't have to worry about you acting like a hero in front of the young lady."

I looked past him toward Abby. The man holding her still had her arms pinned behind her back and a hand over her mouth. She wasn't struggling anymore, but none of the fear had left her eyes.

"I never wanted the money," I said. "That woman gave it to me by mistake."

"It would appear that way," he said. "But that isn't important anymore. All that matters now is that you return what you took."

"Let her go first."

"This isn't a negotiation."

"It is if you want that money."

Victor looked down at the gun in his hand, then leaned in close, whispered, "I don't believe you fully understand the situation here. Don't make me clarify."

I stopped talking.

"Where is the envelope, Nick?"

Victor's voice was cold, and I knew I was taking a risk by not telling him what he wanted to know, but I also knew I didn't have a choice. If I gave in, he'd kill us both, but as long as I had something he needed I had a card to play.

I looked up at Victor and tried to keep my voice from shaking. "Not until you let her go."

Victor sighed. "Unfortunate."

"Let her go, and I'll tell you where the money is," I said. "It's all still there."

Victor stood up, ignoring me, and grabbed the chair. He carried it across the room and set it against the wall by the painting, then he slipped his gun into the back of his belt and turned to face me, silent.

"You don't need her," I said. "She's innocent."

This time Victor smiled. He held his hand out flat, palm up. David stepped forward. He took a black knife from his pocket and unfolded it. The blade was short and sharp and curved like a talon. He placed it handle first in Victor's open palm.

Victor looked down at the knife, then up at David.

David turned to me and swung hard.

The side of his fist connected with the bridge of my nose, slamming my head back. A brilliant cascade of light exploded behind my eyes, blinding me, and sent shards of pain shooting through my head and down my spine.

The room swam around me.

Victor stood across from me, watching, still holding the knife. "It upsets me the way this is turning out," he said. "I had higher hopes."

I coughed, tasted blood.

"Obviously the envelope was delivered to you by accident," Victor said. "I was hoping you'd recognize that fact and return it, but I can see that's not going to be the case."

I tried to say something, anything, but the blood in my throat was thick, making it impossible to speak.

"Unfortunately, your decision has consequences."

I watched him lift the knife, and I bit down on the insides of my cheeks, trying to prepare myself for whatever came next. I waited for him to step closer, but he didn't.

Instead, he crossed the room toward Abby.

When she saw him coming, she lurched backward against the man holding her, fighting against his grip, raging behind his hand.

"Every decision we make has consequences." Victor stopped in front of Abby, then reached out and grabbed the collar of her shirt and pulled it away from her skin. "Action and reaction. It's actually very simple."

He lifted the knife and cut through her collar.

Abby twisted in the man's grip, and for an instant she managed to free herself enough to scream at them, but the man holding her recovered quickly, squeezing her tighter.

"Some people, however, don't grasp the concept of consequences, and I can see now that you're one of those people, Nick." Victor ran the knife down the front of Abby's shirt, cutting through the thin fabric as he spoke. "Everyone knows that if they drive too fast, they might get a ticket. If they drink too much, they'll have a hangover. If they kill someone, they might go to prison. But with the smaller things, people sometimes need a reminder."

When he finished cutting, he reached out and pulled the two sides of Abby's shirt apart, as if opening a set of curtains, revealing her skin and a thin pink bra.

"Wait." My voice was a whisper. "Don't . . ."

He looked back at me.

"Don't get me wrong," he said. "Modification of behavior is fundamental in a civilized society." He tapped the knife in the air, emphasizing his point. "But what happens when the consequences of a person's actions aren't clear? What happens then?"

Victor turned back to Abby.

He pulled the middle of her bra away from her skin and slid the curved blade under the fabric between her breasts.

"How do you make the right decision when you don't understand what's at stake?"

Abby stopped struggling, and from where I sat, I could see the tears running down her face, covering the man's hand over her mouth. She was staring at me over Victor's shoulder, her eyes panicked and desperate.

I wanted to help her, but the ringing in my head was loud, and the floor felt unsteady under my feet. There was nothing I could do.

"The answer, I suppose, is a teacher."

Victor pulled the knife back hard, cutting through the center of Abby's bra, exposing her breasts. Abby cried out, helpless.

I coughed, trying to clear the blood out of my throat.

Victor turned to me, his eyes distant. "And teachers sometimes need to make an example."

He flipped the knife over in his hand, then reached out and grabbed her left nipple and pulled, twisting it hard.

This time when Abby screamed, it was loud.

I saw her legs wobble under her, but the man holding her wouldn't let her fall, and Victor didn't loosen his grip. Instead, he glanced back at me, then twisted harder, straining with the effort.

Abby shrieked. The sound was deafening.

When Victor spoke next, his smile was gone.

"This is your consequence, Nick."

He turned and pressed the edge of the curved blade against the skin above Abby's nipple and began to slice. Abby thrashed against the man holding her, kicking and fighting, screaming.

Finally, I found my voice. It was choked and broken, but it was there.

"My car," I said. "The envelope, it's in my car."

Victor looked back at me. The knife was still pressed against Abby's skin, and I could see a thin trail of blood running down the side of her breast, dripping onto the floor.

"If you're lying to me—"

"I'm not lying," I said. "The envelope is in my car, in the glove compartment. The keys are in my pocket."

Victor nodded to David, who reached into my jacket pocket. He took the keys, then walked out the front door.

Once he was gone, Victor lowered the knife. He let go of Abby, then reached out and gently closed her shirt over her chest, covering her. He looked up at the man behind her and said something I didn't hear.

The man stepped back, and Abby crumpled to the floor, sobbing, trying to cover herself with her torn shirt.

Victor turned to me, shook his head.

"I do hope you're telling the truth," he said. "I can't stand the sight of blood."

13

For a while the only sound in the room came from Abby, crying in the corner. Victor didn't seem to notice. He sat next to me on the couch, knife in hand, staring at me.

I tried to not let it bother me.

I don't know how much time passed before I heard David's footsteps on the porch. When he came back inside, he had the manila envelope in one hand and a black laptop bag slung over his shoulder. He handed the envelope to Victor and tossed my keys on my lap. They hit my leg and dropped to the floor.

Victor opened the envelope and looked inside.

"It's all in there," I said. "Everything she gave me, just like I told you."

He ignored me and reached into the envelope. He took out the flash drive and handed it to David.

David slipped the bag off his shoulder, then pulled out a laptop and opened it on the coffee table. He plugged the flash drive into the side and started typing.

"It's password protected," I said. "You won't be able to open it without—"

"I'm in," David said.

Victor got up and walked around to the other side of the coffee table. He leaned over David, their faces reflecting the dead blue light from the screen.

"Is it all there?"

"I think so," David said. "Give me a minute."

Victor stood and paced the room, tapping the blade of the knife against his open palm. After the second pass, he started mumbling to himself, his eyes distant and unfocused.

The zip tie around my wrists was cutting off my circulation, and my hands were going numb. I tried to move them enough to get the blood flowing, but that only made it worse.

"You've got what you wanted," I said. "Untie me."

Victor continued to pace the room. If he heard what I said, he didn't show it.

Several minutes passed before David stopped typing. "It's incomplete."

Victor stepped behind him and leaned in to look. "Are you sure?"

David nodded. "I'm sure."

"Check again," Victor said. "Maybe she—"

"There's nothing to check," David said. "It's not here. She lied to us."

Victor stared at the screen for a moment, then stood and ran his hand through his hair. He turned and threw the knife against the wall. It hit hard, cracking the plaster.

Abby flinched, pushing herself back into the corner.

After that, the room was silent.

Victor stood with his back to me, and I could see his shoulders rising and falling with each breath. The mood in the room was changing, and I didn't like it.

"That's what she gave me," I said. "I didn't touch—"

Victor held up one finger, signaling for me to stop talking, but I couldn't do it. I wanted him to know.

"I didn't touch anything," I said. "If there's a problem, it's because she didn't—"

"Mr. Ellis?"

The man standing next to Abby looked over at Victor.

"Pick that up." Victor pointed to the knife lying on the floor next to several shards of broken plaster. "If this one says one more word, I want you to cut his fucking tongue out of his head."

Ellis nodded, then bent down and picked up the knife.

I looked over at Abby and started to say something else, but then her eyes went wide and she shook her head.

I changed my mind.

"You know what?" Victor turned and looked from me to Abby, then back to me. "On second thought, shoot them both."

At first the words didn't sink in, but then Ellis reached into his coat and pulled out a black handgun. As he started toward me, the reality of the situation hit hard. It was like a stopwatch inside my head counting down.

In the distance, I heard Abby begging Victor to stop, but all I could see was Ellis and the gun. I tried to think of something to say, but there was nothing.

Ellis stood in front of me and lifted the gun.

I closed my eyes.

"Wait."

This time it was Victor's voice, and when I opened my eyes he was staring at Abby. She was standing next to him, holding her shirt closed with both hands and shifting her weight from one foot to the other, back and forth.

"Say that again," Victor said. "What you told me."

I saw Abby's lip tremble, but when she spoke her voice was steady. "I said we'd talk to her. We'll get whatever she owes you. Just stop, please."

Victor turned to Ellis and shook his head.

Ellis lowered the gun.

I felt a cold chill drip down my spine, and I started to shake.

I couldn't make it stop.

Victor stared at Abby. "What makes you think she'll do anything for you?"

"Not me," Abby said. "Him."

She nodded toward me.

Victor looked at me. "Him?"

"He has to meet with her again," she said. "He's the only one she's seen. If anyone else shows up, she'll know something went wrong and she'll get scared. She'll close up, and then you'll never get whatever it is you're after."

Victor seemed to consider this, silent.

"She's a liar, but she's not stupid," Abby said. "If you want to get what she owes you, it has to be him."

"And then what?"

"And then you let us go."

Victor looked down at me on the couch. "What do you have to say about all of this?"

I didn't want to say anything, but I saw what Abby was doing, and I understood. She was terrified, but she was also thinking on her feet. I had no intention of helping them, but lying might buy us some time.

"I'll do what I can."

Victor frowned. "That doesn't sound convincing."

Abby stared at me over his shoulder, pleading.

I took a deep breath and tried to steady my voice. It worked, but barely.

"I'll get you what you want," I said. "If you let us go."

Victor turned and pointed to the laptop. David pulled the flash drive and handed it to him. Victor crossed the room and held it up in front of me and said, "You give this to her and tell her she has one chance to deliver what we agreed upon." He paused. "Threaten her if you have to—I don't care—but get her to deliver. Do you understand?"

"I understand."

"Be convincing," he said. "Otherwise, we do this again. And next time we'll include your wife."

I looked up fast—too fast.

Victor noticed and smiled. "What we do to her will be worse than anything you can imagine."

I felt the rage building inside me, but I forced it down. My hands were tied and I was outnumbered. There was nothing I could do, at least not yet.

"She's not part of this," I said. "Don't—"

"You've made her a part of this." He held the flash drive up one more time, then set it next to me on the couch. "If you try to run or if you talk to the police, I'm going to take your wife apart piece by piece."

He reached out and set his hand on my shoulder. It took all my strength not to shrug him off.

Victor motioned to David and Ellis, then turned to Abby. He took a white business card from his pocket and set it on the coffee table.

"You have twenty-four hours to get the information we want, no longer. Once you have it, call this number and leave a message. We'll come to you."

She nodded and backed away from him.

David put the laptop back in the bag, then picked up the envelope and handed it to Victor before following Ellis out the front door. Victor stayed behind. He stared at the envelope in his hand, then looked up at me before dropping it on the couch.

"For your trouble."

He walked out, closing the door behind him.

I looked over at Abby, leaning against the wall. Once the door closed the tears came in a flood, and she slid down to the floor, trembling.

I turned away.

14

Abby disappeared into the bedroom.

When she came back, she was wearing a long pink T-shirt and carrying a pair of scissors.

"Turn around."

She cut through the plastic zip tie around my wrists. Once my hands were free, I shook them out to get the blood flowing, then took my cell phone from my pocket and dialed Kara's number.

"Do you want some ice for your nose?"

"I'm fine."

Abby dropped the scissors on the coffee table next to Victor's card and sat on the couch. She leaned forward, rubbing the sides of her head with her fingertips, mumbling to herself.

Kara's phone went to voice mail. I hung up and dialed her number again.

It occurred to me that she was screening my calls, and after our conversation that morning it didn't surprise me. Kara was upset, and usually I'd take a step back and give her the space she needed to calm down, but not this time.

When her voice mail picked up again, I turned away from Abby and pressed the phone against my ear and said, "Kara, call me as soon as you get this. It's important."

I thought about adding more, but I didn't know where to start, and with Abby sitting a few feet away it didn't seem like the time.

I hung up, slipped the phone into my pocket, and turned to Abby on the couch.

"Are you okay?"

She nodded, didn't look up.

I walked over and started searching the ground around the couch for my keys. I found them, then went to the window and split the blinds with two fingers and looked out at the empty street.

I didn't see anyone, but that didn't mean anything.

"Are they still out there?"

"Doesn't look like it." I stepped away from the window, letting the blinds clap shut. "The street's clear."

The manila envelope and the flash drive were both on the couch next to Abby. I put the flash drive back in the envelope, slid it into my pocket, and then flipped through my keys.

Abby watched me. "What are you doing?"

"I'm going to find my wife."

"You're leaving?"

Her voice was gentle and quiet, and it touched something inside of me that I wished wasn't there.

"I need to make sure she's okay."

"Please don't leave me here," she said. "I don't want to be here alone."

"I'm sorry. I have to go."

I started for the door, but Abby stopped me.

"Wait." She took a few quick steps toward me, stopping just out of reach. "Let me come with you."

The way she looked at me made it hard to say no, but then I thought of Kara and how she'd react if I showed up at her house with a twenty-year-old blonde in tow.

"That's not the best idea," I said. "Is there someplace else you can go? I'll take you wherever you—"

"Please?" Abby stared up at me, her lips trembling. "They could still be out there. They might . . ." Her voice broke, and she stopped talking.

"Is there anyone you can call?"

She shook her head. "I don't have anyone here."

"What about a neighbor?"

Abby looked away, and I could tell she was trying to hold back tears. It was a fight she was losing, and when they came, they came hard.

I wasn't sure what to do.

I checked my watch, frowned, stepped closer.

"It's okay," I said. "Everything is going to be fine."

I reached out and put my hand on her shoulder. When I touched her, she turned fast and wrapped her arms around me and squeezed, tucking herself against my chest.

She stayed like that, shaking, crying.

Eventually, I gave in.

———

The street outside was quiet and calm, and as we walked along the sidewalk, a warm lilac breeze moved with us. Abby held my arm tight in hers, and she kept her head down the entire way.

"I'm parked up here," I said. "It's not far."

She nodded, walked faster.

When we got to the car, I opened the passenger door, and Abby slid in without a word. I went around to the driver's side, then stopped and scanned the street. The black SUV was gone, but I still couldn't shake the feeling that someone was watching us. I stood by the car, searching, but eventually I gave up and climbed in.

Abby was tucked down in the passenger seat. She wasn't crying anymore, and that was good, but she also wasn't talking, and that worried me.

"You doing okay?"

"I'll be fine." She had her arms folded gently over her chest, and she didn't look at me as she spoke. "Can we get away from here, please?"

I started the engine.

Five minutes later we were on the highway heading south to Kara's house. I took the cell phone from my pocket and tried calling her one more time, but once again there was no answer.

When I hung up, I saw that Abby was crying.

"Hey," I said. "We'll figure this out."

"Will we?"

"Of course," I said. "We'll get out of this, find someplace safe. It'll be okay."

Abby nodded, looked away.

"We'll work it out, I promise."

"I just don't understand." She ran her fingers under her eyes, then wiped them on her jeans. "I've never done anything to that woman. Why would she send those men to my house? Why would she have them . . . ?"

Her voice cracked and she turned away, staring out at the city lights passing outside her window. She didn't say anything else, and for a long time we drove in silence.

I didn't mind.

There was nothing I could say to her that would make her feel better, and I had other things to think about.

What was I going to say to Kara?

Keeping her out of this was no longer an option. They knew who she was. They'd threatened her directly, and she deserved to know what was going on. I had to tell her the truth about everything, even if it meant killing what little trust she had left in me.

I couldn't see any other choice.

As I drove I went over everything that'd happened at Abby's house. I tried to make sense of it, but the more I thought about it, the more confused I felt.

Nothing added up, and I knew something was wrong.

I looked over at Abby. She was leaning against the passenger door with her eyes closed, but I didn't think she was sleeping.

"Why didn't they take the money?"

Abby opened her eyes slowly. "What?"

"There's twenty thousand dollars in that envelope," I said. "Why didn't they take it?"

She sat up, stretched. "Why does it matter?"

"Because it doesn't fit," I said. "Nobody hands over that kind of cash. I don't care who you are."

"I really don't know."

"Me neither," I said. "But it makes me wonder."

"About what?"

I paused. "About what's on that flash drive."

15

Kara lived on the outskirts of Ponca Hills in the house we bought together. I hadn't been back since the separation, and when I pulled up out front the memories of our time there came flooding in.

I parked along the sidewalk, then leaned over to look up at the house. Kara's car wasn't in the driveway, and the windows were dark.

"Is this it?" Abby asked.

I told her it was, then shut off the engine and opened the door. The overhead light came on, bright, and I reached up and shut it off.

"I'll be right back. This shouldn't take long."

Abby sat up. "I'm coming, too."

Before I could argue, she opened the passenger door and got out. I watched her take a pink hair tie from her pocket and pull her hair into a ponytail.

She leaned into the car. "You don't mind, right?"

I frowned, got out of the car, and walked around to the sidewalk. I tried to think of a way to get her to stay, but I couldn't, and I didn't think it would matter anyway.

She was coming.

Showing up at Kara's unannounced was one thing. Showing up unannounced with a young blonde was completely different, and I didn't see any way that it would end well. Then again, considering what I had to tell her, I didn't think anything could make the situation worse.

"If you're going to come along, don't say anything. Let me do the talking."

"Fine, as long as I'm not out here alone."

I told her I understood, and it was the truth. After everything she'd been through, I didn't blame her.

———

Kara's house—our house—was a two-story brick Tudor that was framed with juniper bushes and a tall wooden fence surrounding the backyard. There was a stone stepping path leading to the front of the house, and as we walked along it, I glanced up at the arched window on the second level.

At one time that'd been my office, and it was where I'd done most of my work. I'd had a desk at the *Tribune*, but everything that mattered had been done in that one room behind that black window.

When we got to the front door, I reached out and rang the bell.

Abby straightened herself and brushed her hands over the front of her shirt. She took a deep breath and let it out slow, then looked at me and tried to smile.

"You're fine," I said. "Just let me talk to her."

"What do you think she's going to say?"

"No idea."

I knew exactly what Kara was going to say, but I kept that to myself. Abby had been through enough, and I didn't see any reason to worry her more.

Except no one answered.

I rang the bell again.

Abby moved to the window and tried to see inside. "I don't think she's home."

"I'll go around back and check the door," I said. "Wait here. I'll be—"

Abby moved first, cutting in front of me and walking around to the wooden fence alongside of the house.

I shook my head and followed.

We stopped at the gate, and I flipped the metal latch and pushed it open. We went through and followed another stone stepping path around to the backyard.

Abby went up the porch steps to the door.

"It's locked."

I stayed in the yard and looked around. There was a bed of river rocks bordering the porch, and I scraped my foot across the surface, moving the rocks, searching. When I found the one I was looking for, I picked it up.

"What are you doing?"

There was a plastic plug on the bottom of the rock. I pulled it out and shook the rock over my hand. A silver key dropped into my palm.

"Are you sure that's a good idea?" she asked. "If she's not home, we should wait and try calling again."

I went up the steps to the back door and slid the key into the lock. It turned, and I pushed the door open.

The house was quiet.

"Kara?"

There was no answer.

I replaced the key in the false rock and tossed it over the side of the porch.

"Nick, are you sure about this?"

I told her that it was fine, then pushed the door the rest of the way open.

"Anyone home?"

The back door opened into a mudroom just off the kitchen. I moved slowly, listening, but the only sounds I heard were the low breath of the furnace fan and the rhythmic ticking of the wall clock.

"We shouldn't be in here."

"I'm going to look around," I said. "You can wait in the car if you like."

Abby exhaled loud and stepped inside. I could tell she wanted to say more, but to her credit she didn't.

I walked the rest of the way through the kitchen and out into the dining room and the living room beyond. This was the first time I'd been in the house since I'd moved out, and the familiarity of it was hard. Some of the furniture had been moved, and there were a few new photographs on the mantel above the fireplace, but other than that it was all exactly how I remembered.

I let the memories fill me.

"I don't like this," Abby said. "We should go."

"In a minute."

I crossed the living room toward the open arch leading to the bedrooms and the bathroom. I went through them one by one before stopping in the bedroom.

It was hard to stay focused.

Kara and I had been separated for a while, but part of me still thought of this place as home. Except it wasn't. This was Kara's house.

"Nick, we really shouldn't—"

"I know." My voice came out harsher than I'd intended, and Abby took a step back. I saw a flash of fear on her face, and I held up my hands. "Just give me a minute."

"Okay," she said. "But we're in your ex-wife's house, and she's not here. That's bad."

"She's not my ex-wife," I said. "We're separated."

"That doesn't make it any better."

I felt another twinge of anger, but it faded.

She was right. This was bad, but I didn't care. After everything that'd happened, I wasn't leaving until I knew that her house was safe.

"I'm going to check upstairs."

"Wait, Nick—"

"They were in my apartment last night and I didn't know it," I said. "I'm not leaving here until I've looked around."

"But—"

"You wanted to come along," I said. "This is what I'm doing. If you're uncomfortable, wait in the car."

Abby didn't say anything else. She just stood there, staring at me with her mouth open as if I'd slapped her.

"I'm going to check the rest of the house."

I turned and started for the stairs.

"If you really want to help her, we need to talk to Patricia."

"Talk to Patricia?"

"It's the only way we're going to get out of this."

"I'm not talking to anyone," I said. "I'm going to tell Kara what happened and convince her to leave with me."

"You told him you'd fix this."

"I told him what he wanted to hear to keep them from killing us both," I said. "I don't know what was supposed to be on that flash drive, but considering what he was willing to do to get it, I don't want any part of it."

Abby stared at me. "They'll kill you."

"We'll see."

"What are you going to do?"

I stood there for a moment and thought about my answer. I didn't know what I was going to do, not until I talked to Kara. Until then it was one step at a time.

"Right now?" I motioned toward the stairs leading to the second floor. "I'm going to check upstairs."

Abby didn't say anything else.

I turned away, but then I heard footsteps on the porch and the delicate chime of keys in the lock.

I stopped, and everything inside me went cold.

Abby's eyes were wide. She ran to where I was standing and grabbed my arm. "We have to go."

I pulled my arm away, waited.

The door opened, and Kara stepped inside, her silhouette filling the doorway. I knew I should say something to warn her, but before I could she reached out and flipped the light switch.

It was too late.

16

W hat the hell is this?"

Kara stood in the doorway. I moved toward her.

"You didn't answer your phone," I said. "I—"

"Did you break into my house?"

"We need to talk," I said. "This is important."

Kara stared at me, and I could feel the tension building in the room. I tried to think of something to say, but then Kara looked past me toward Abby.

"Who is this?"

"This is Abigail Pierce," I said. "She's involved."

"Involved?"

Kara closed her eyes, then pressed her hands together in front of her mouth, as if in prayer. When she spoke next, her voice was a whisper.

"Nick?"

I stepped closer. "Yeah?"

"Get out of my house."

"Kara—"

"Get out." She opened her eyes, stared at me. "Now."

I didn't move.

"I mean it, Nick."

"I can't," I said. "We need to talk."

"Do I need to call the cops?"

I turned to Abby. "Will you give us a minute?"

Abby nodded and started for the kitchen.

"Wrong way, sweetheart." Kara moved away from the front door, clearing a path. "Out, both of you."

"I'm not leaving until you hear what I have to say."

"And what's that, Nick?" She folded her arms over her chest. "Are you going to ask me to run away with you again, or are you going to explain why you and Bubbles here broke into my house?"

"You don't understand."

"No, I don't care. There's a difference." She waved a hand in the air between us. "This—you being here—is not acceptable."

"I can explain if you'd listen to me."

"There's nothing you can say to me that I haven't heard from you before."

"You might be surprised."

Kara stopped talking, shook her head. "I can't believe you broke into my house. This is low, Nick, even for you."

The tone of her voice was harsh, and I could feel the frustration building inside me. I tried to push it away, but it didn't work.

"My name is still on the goddamn title, Kara."

"You're right," she said. "Maybe *that's* something we should talk about."

Abby inched forward and motioned toward the front door. "I think I'll wait out on the porch."

"Not just you," Kara said, never taking her eyes off me. "I want you both gone now, or the next time you and I talk about anything it'll be through a lawyer."

For a moment we just stared at each other, and neither of us moved.

Abby slipped between us and walked outside.

Once she was gone, Kara shook her head.

"Is this what you're doing now?"

"What's that?"

"I won't run away to Mexico with you, so you bring a child to my house?"

"She's not a child."

"You're a little young for a midlife crisis, so what exactly are you trying to prove?"

I felt my muscles get tight, and I stepped closer.

Kara backed up against the wall. "Don't touch me, Nick."

I didn't touch her, but I didn't let her move, either. I understood why she was angry, but this had gone on long enough. I pressed my hands against the wall on either side of her head and leaned in.

"Someone wanted to kill the two of us tonight, and they almost did."

Kara watched me as I spoke, silent.

"I talked my way out of it, but now they want me to do something for them that I don't want to do. And if I don't do it, they're going to come back, and this time I won't be able to talk my way out of it."

Kara's eyes narrowed. "What did you do, Nick?"

I took a deep breath, exhaled slow. "I pretended to be someone else."

"What?"

"It's not important right now," I said. "I'm here because they broke into my apartment last night, and now they know about you."

I saw a flash of fear pass over Kara's face, but then it was gone as quickly as it'd come.

"Jesus."

She put her hands on my chest and tried to push me away, but I didn't move.

"I want you to stay at Charlie's tonight."

"Absolutely not."

"It's not safe here," I said. "At least if you're there I'll know you're okay."

Kara smiled, then reached up and touched the side of my face with her fingertips. She moved them slowly across my cheek to my lips, then leaned in and whispered.

"I don't care what you want," she said, her breath warm on my skin. "Now get the fuck out of my house."

———

We drove for a long time, and Abby didn't say a word until we were far away from Kara's place.

That was a good thing.

I needed time, and Abby somehow understood.

It wasn't until we were back on the highway, where the only sounds were the low drone of the engine and the wind passing outside, that I started to relax.

I hated the idea of leaving Kara alone, but she didn't want my help, and there was nothing I could do to change her mind. I didn't blame her, either. Everything I touched fell apart, and no one knew that better than her.

Still, I wasn't ready to give up.

I'd bought some time with Victor, and I could try talking to Kara again in the morning after she'd had a chance to calm down. If I told her everything that'd happened, and if she saw the danger she was in, maybe she'd change her mind about leaving.

"Are you taking me home?"

I glanced over at Abby in the passenger seat. "Is that where you want to go?"

She shook her head. "No."

I checked my watch. It was late, and my options were limited.

"I can find you a hotel." I paused. "Or you can stay at my place. It's small, but the couch is comfortable."

"You don't mind?"

I wasn't sure how I felt about her staying with me, but I kept that to myself.

"No," I said. "I don't mind."

Abby smiled and eased back in the seat. She was quiet for a while. Then she turned to me and said, "I'm sorry about your wife. That could've gone better."

"There's a lot behind what you saw," I said. "Things haven't been easy between us for a long time."

"She was really angry."

"That's my fault," I said. "It was stupid of me to go over there. I should've listened to you."

"At least you see it now."

I laughed, but when I looked over at Abby, her eyes were closed and her face was blank. I watched the shadows from the streetlights pass over her, dark then light then dark again, before turning back and looking out at the road ahead.

We drove the rest of the way in silence.

17

I pulled up to my apartment and parked along the street out front. Abby and I went through the double doors and into the lobby. She stopped next to the elevators and looked around at the plastic plants and the thin, cushioned couch and chair along the far wall.

I pushed the call button and waited.

"This is a nice place," she said. "You made it sound like some kind of rooming house."

"It's cheap."

Abby shrugged. "I've lived in worse."

Something about the way she said it made me feel bad for complaining, and I let the subject drop.

The elevator doors opened and we stepped inside. I pushed the button for the third floor, then leaned against the wall as the doors slid shut.

"Does that hurt?" Abby touched the bridge of her nose with her finger. "It doesn't look so good."

I reached up and felt the sides of my nose. It was swollen, but there was no pain, so I didn't think it was broken.

"It's fine," I said. "Not the first time."

"Not the first time you've been hit in the face?"

"I used to get into fights as a kid." I tilted my head down and pointed out a few old scars. "That's why I'm so pretty."

Abby leaned in for a closer look, then touched one of the scars under my eye with her thumb. Her skin felt warm and soft against mine, and I held my breath.

"There's nothing wrong with the way you look."

I laughed.

"What's so funny?"

I shook my head, didn't answer.

She started to push, but then the elevator doors opened and I stepped out, ending the conversation.

"Come on," I said. "I'm at the far end."

Abby followed me down the hall to my apartment. I unlocked the door and held it open for her. She walked in and looked around.

"This is cute." She turned to face me. "I can't believe you don't like it."

Before I could say anything, she crossed the room toward the windows along the far wall.

"Oh my God, look at your view."

I took off my coat and draped it over the arm of the couch, then walked up and stood next to her and looked out over the city skyline and the shadowed stretch of mountains along the horizon.

"It's so pretty," she said.

"You should see the sunsets."

Abby stood at the window, the reflection of the city in her eyes. "I'd live here just for this view."

"One good thing doesn't outweigh the bad," I said. "I like it here, but it's not home."

Abby turned to me. "Where's home?"

I shrugged, didn't answer.

"With your wife?"

"At one time," I said. "Now I'm not so sure."

Abby stared at me, and for a moment I thought she was going to say more, but she just looked away.

"That's a bigger story," I said.

"I'm sorry, it's none of my business."

She was right, but at that moment I didn't care.

I motioned to the kitchen. "Do you want a drink?"

She shrugged. "Why not?"

I walked into the kitchen and took two glasses from the cabinet, along with a half-empty bottle of Macallan. I carried everything back to the living room.

Abby was still at the window.

I set the glasses on the coffee table, then reached for my coat. I picked it up off the couch and felt the weight of the manila envelope in my pocket. I took it out, unfolded it, and then set it on the coffee table next to my glass.

My head was beginning to ache, low and dull. I closed my eyes and touched the bridge of my nose.

"Are you okay?"

When I opened my eyes, Abby was coming around the coffee table. She sat at the other end of the couch, one leg folded under her.

I told her I was fine, then reached for the bottle, pulled the cap, and poured.

"You don't look fine."

"It's been a bad day."

Abby made a dismissive noise. "Tell me about it."

I smiled, held up my drink. "To better ones."

She touched her glass to mine and we drank.

For a while we were both quiet. I leaned back on the couch and thought about Kara. For the first time I let myself consider the idea of leaving without her. I wanted to believe that there was still a chance we could start over, but the more I thought about it, the more I wondered if I was kidding myself.

I turned to Abby. She was staring out at nothing and absently running her thumb along the side of her glass.

I finished my drink, then poured another.

"Tell me about yourself," I said. "Do you have a boyfriend?"

Abby looked up and smiled. "Really?"

"Sorry." I cringed. "I'm not very good at small talk."

Abby laughed. "No, no boyfriend."

"Good for you. Men are a mess."

"People are a mess." She finished her drink, held the glass out. "Every last one of them."

I frowned, then took the bottle and refilled her glass. "You're too young to be that cynical."

"Age doesn't matter," she said. "Once you've seen how the machine works, you can't unsee it."

"And you've seen how the machine works?"

I was smiling when I said it, but when Abby looked up at me, something cold passed behind her eyes, and I stopped.

Abby must've noticed, because she laughed and took a drink, and whatever I'd seen in her eyes disappeared behind the sound.

"I've got a question for you," she said. "You don't have to answer if you don't want."

"One more drink and I'll probably tell you anything."

"Is that right?" She reached for the bottle and topped off my drink. "In that case, tell me what happened between you and your wife."

"Wow."

Abby smiled.

I sat there for a minute, thinking, not saying a word. Then I took a drink and eased back against the cushions.

"I'll make you a deal," I said. "I'll answer your question if you answer one of mine."

"What's your question?"

"I don't know yet. I'll have to think of one."

Abby stared at me, shrugged. "Sure, why not? But you first. Why did you two split up?"

"You really want to hear about that?"

"We did just make a deal, didn't we?"

"I guess we did."

I thought about my answer. I didn't mind telling her about Kara and me, but my head felt light and warm from the scotch, and it took a minute to get started.

"Poker."

A line formed between her eyebrows. "Cards?"

"I lost a lot of money, all of it Kara's."

"How much?"

"Ten thousand dollars," I said. "Not huge, but not nothing, either. It was our entire savings. Definitely more than I could replace working as a desk writer for the *Tribune*."

"And that's why she left you?"

"It wasn't the first time I'd screwed up," I said. "I'd had bad beats before. This time she'd had enough."

"I'm sorry."

"Everyone has their breaking point, and that was hers." I lifted my hands and looked around my apartment. "Now I'm here."

"Now we're here." Abby smiled at me, bit her lower lip. "It's funny how things work out, don't you think?"

I felt a twinge, and I tried to ignore it.

"Okay," I said. "Your turn."

She sat up. "I'm ready."

"Tell me about you," I said. "Where did you grow up?"

"All over," she said. "My mother kept us moving, the South mostly, then the West Coast. We spent a year in Alaska. That was my favorite."

"You liked the cold?"

"I liked the solitude," she said. "The fewer people around, the better things usually are."

I didn't know what to say to that, so I looked down at my glass and the light reflecting gold off the amber.

"How did your mother die?"

I felt Abby stiffen across from me, and I immediately regretted the question.

"I'm sorry, I—"

"You said one question."

"You're right, I did."

Abby didn't say anything else, and I finished my drink, cursing myself under my breath for being me.

"We should get some sleep, anyway." I set my empty glass on the coffee table and pointed to a door by the kitchen. "There's the bathroom. I'll get you a pillow."

"Thanks."

I grabbed the manila envelope off the table, then got up and went into my bedroom. The scotch was spinning through me, and I stood for a moment, letting the room settle. Once it did I walked around my bed and opened the drawer on the bedside table. I slipped the manila envelope inside, then crossed the room to the closet. I took two blankets and an extra pillow off the top shelf, then went back into the living room and set them on the couch.

I could hear water running in the bathroom.

"It can get cold in here," I said. "So I brought you an extra blanket. If you need more, just knock."

I turned toward the bathroom.

The door was open and Abby was inside, standing with her back to me. Her shirt was off, and she was staring at herself in the mirror, examining her left breast. The skin around her nipple was torn and bruised black.

I stood there, watching.

Abby noticed, and she looked up at me in the mirror.

For a moment neither of us moved. I knew I should say something or at least be a gentleman and look away, but I couldn't do either.

Abby turned and faced me.

She didn't speak, and she didn't try to cover herself. Instead, she stared at me, half smiling, then reached out slowly and closed the door.

I stood there for a while longer before walking back to my bedroom with my heart pounding hard in my chest.

It was a long time before I slept.

18

In the dream I'm drowning.

   Spinning in black water.

Choking.

I fight and open my eyes. I'm in bed, and my room is filled with swirling gray shadows. I hear rain falling outside, and several dim flashes of lightning spark behind the curtains.

I focus on the sound of the rain and try to force myself to wake up, but the harder I try, the deeper I go.

Drowning forever.

And I'm not alone.

Someone is standing in the doorway—a figure, clean and dark, silhouetted against the gray.

A pulse of fear starts in the center of my chest and builds, spreading through me like a fire. I try to sit up, try to say something, but my throat closes over the words and nothing comes out.

The figure in the doorway doesn't move.

I close my eyes.

Wake up!

I hear movement, a series of rapid clicks, like claws scuttling across hardwood, and I open my eyes.

The figure is gone.

At first I don't see it. Then I do, crouched at the foot of my bed, a shadow among shadows.

The panic burns through me.

Wake up! Wake up! Wake—

I watch as the figure slides along the floor, inching closer, and then rises up until it's leaning over me. I can feel its breath on my skin, wet and rank. Then I see its face, worn features carved into cold flesh, dark-socketed eyes the color of bad dreams.

I can't look away.

And it watches me as I scream.

———

I sat up, my heart racing, the dream still fresh.

I put a hand to my chest and looked around the room, trying to steady myself. I was in my bed, and the sunlight shone warm through a break in the curtains.

I was alone.

I sat there for a while, waiting for the dream to fade. Then I got up, put on my clothes, and walked out into the living room.

The sun was bright, and the air smelled like bacon and fresh coffee. Abby was in the kitchen, singing along to the radio. The blankets she'd used the night before were folded and stacked on the couch, along with her jeans and shoes.

I walked around to the kitchen. Abby was holding a spatula and dancing along to the oldies station—LaVern Baker singing "Bumble Bee." She was wearing her pink T-shirt from the night before, and the bottom barely touched the tops of her thighs.

When she saw me, she jumped, laughed.

"You scared me."

"What are you doing?"

"Making breakfast." Abby turned back to the stove and the bacon popping in the skillet. "It's about ready. Are you hungry?"

I didn't answer her right away. All I could do was stand there and watch. Part of me thought I should ask her to get dressed, but it was a small part and easy to ignore.

"I could eat."

"Great." Abby reached over and shut off the radio. "I hope you don't mind, but I woke up in the best mood, and when I'm in a good mood, I want to cook."

"I'm surprised you found anything to make."

"You had more than you think," she said, flipping the bacon in the skillet. "It won't be the best meal you'll ever eat, but that's okay."

Abby's voice was bright, and I stood there, watching her as she moved through my kitchen.

"Why are you in such a good mood?"

"Because I figured it out." She turned and faced me, leaning her hip against the counter. "I know what we're going to do. I have the answer."

I didn't say anything.

Abby smiled. "You didn't forget, did you?"

"I didn't forget, but—"

"I fell asleep last night with nothing, and when I woke up this morning it was all there—all of it." She turned back to the stove. "I figured out how you can talk to Patricia without raising suspicions."

I kept quiet.

The last thing I was going to do was stick around and be a pawn for Victor. I might be in deep, but that didn't mean I had to go deeper.

I started to tell this to Abby, but she stopped me and motioned to the cabinet.

"Can you grab a couple plates?"

I opened the cabinet and took down two plates. Abby spread the cooked bacon out over a fold of paper towels, then went to the refrigerator and found a half-empty carton of eggs.

"Coffee's ready if you want to—"

"Listen," I said. "We should talk."

Abby looked up at me, and I saw a shade of worry in her eyes, but it didn't last. "We will. Just let me finish this first."

I wanted to insist, but it'd been a while since I'd eaten, and the smell of bacon was making it hard to concentrate on anything else. I gave in and took two coffee cups from the cabinet and set them on the table. When I stepped back, I noticed my phone on the counter, and I picked it up.

There was a message from Charlie.

"Shit."

"Something wrong?"

"No." I slid the phone into my pocket. "I told someone I'd call, and I forgot."

"You've got a few minutes before breakfast is ready."

"This'll take longer than a few minutes," I said. "I'll call him later."

Abby cracked a few eggs into the skillet and splashed the tops with grease until they turned white. Then she set them on the plates and added the bacon.

"I didn't find any bread, so no toast." She put the skillet in the sink and picked up the plates and handed one to me. "This'll have to do."

It looked great, and I told her so.

She smiled, and we sat at the table.

Abby took a small bite of the bacon, then leaned back in her chair and said, "Do you want to hear it?"

"Hear what?"

"My plan," she said. "With Patricia."

"About that." I took a bite, then another, chewing as I spoke. "Like I told you last night, as soon as I talk to Kara I'm leaving, one way or the other."

"I know," she said. "But just hear me out. I don't know why I didn't think of this before, but Daniel came home from the hospital last week."

"I thought he . . ."

"He wanted to go home. I don't blame him. Nobody wants to die in a hospital." Abby picked up her fork, then set it down again. "I haven't gone to see him yet."

I thought I knew where she was going, but I waited for her to say it. I didn't wait long.

"You can come with me," she said. "Patricia will be there. She has no idea who you really are or that we—"

"No."

Abby stared at me. "Why not?"

"Because I'm not going to help those people," I said. "That's insane."

"But . . ." Abby stumbled over her words. "You have to."

I shook my head, then scraped the last of the eggs onto my fork and took a bite. "I don't think I do."

"But, Nick—"

"We don't even know what they're after." I dropped my fork on the plate and leaned forward. "They could be trying to get launch codes or instructions on how to build a dirty bomb for all we know."

"From Patricia?"

"You're missing my point," I said. "Whatever is on that flash drive, I'm sure it's not legal. If my choices are to do nothing and risk them killing me, or do what they ask and spend the rest of my life in prison, then I'm going with the third option."

"What's the third option?"

I stood and picked up my plate. "Leave."

Abby watched me as I walked into the kitchen and set my plate in the sink, but she didn't say anything. When she did speak again, her voice trembled.

"They'll kill you."

"We'll see."

"They'll kill me," she said. "You saw what they were going to do last night. I can't—"

"Then you should leave, too."

"I don't have anywhere to go."

I didn't understand. She was young, she had money, and she was about to inherit a lot more. Any way I looked at the situation, it seemed that all her problems were about to take care of themselves.

"You said something about Iowa."

"Nebraska."

"Okay then, Nebraska."

Abby frowned. "You don't understand. I can't—"

There was a knock at the door, and Abby looked up at me, her eyes wide.

"Were you—?"

I held up my hand, stopping her, and then looked around the kitchen and took a steak knife from the rack next to the stove.

"Stay here."

I walked across the living room to the door, looked through the viewer, and felt my breath catch in my throat.

Kara was standing in the hallway.

19

I turned the bolt and opened the door.

Kara was wearing a green raincoat, and she had her hands in her pockets. When she saw me, she attempted a smile, but it didn't quite work.

"Hey, Nick." She slid a loose strand of hair behind her ear. "I thought we should talk."

I recognized the tone in her voice, and the excitement I'd felt when I saw her standing in the hallway faded fast.

"About last night," I said. "I owe you an apology."

She started to say something, but I stopped her. There was so much I wanted to say, and I was afraid that if I didn't get it all out I'd lose my chance.

"I shouldn't have gone to the house," I said. "But a lot has happened that you need to know about. If you let me explain, I'll tell you everything."

"You don't have to."

"I think I do," I said. "If we're going to make this work, we need to be honest about everything."

"Nick, please stop."

"You don't want to hear it?"

Kara sighed and looked down the hallway toward the elevators, then back at me. "Can I come in?"

I started to say yes, but then I remembered Abby and hesitated. Kara noticed and her eyes narrowed.

"Is there a problem?"

"No, no problem." I looked back into my apartment. Abby was standing in the archway by the kitchen, and all at once her T-shirt seemed even shorter. "Come in, but this isn't what it looks like."

Kara leaned to the side and looked past me into the apartment. I watched the softness in her face turn solid.

"Jesus, Nick." Kara shook her head and started walking back down the hall toward the elevators.

"Kara, wait." I turned back to Abby and spoke slowly. "Get dressed."

Abby nodded.

I ran out into the hallway and caught up with Kara halfway to the elevators. "Hold on a minute."

I reached for her arm, and she pulled away.

"She slept on the couch," I said. "I didn't want to bring her here, but I couldn't leave her alone. She was terrified, and she didn't have anyplace else to go."

Kara kept walking.

"If you don't believe me, call Charlie. He knows what's going on. He'll tell you everything."

"I'm not calling Charlie."

"These people," I said. "You have no idea what they were going to do to her."

"I don't care, Nick."

"You should, because you're involved in this, too."

Kara turned on me. "I'm pregnant."

At first I didn't understand.

The words made sense, but the meaning was lost. When it finally hit, I felt a sudden rush of joy and terror.

Then I did the math.

Kara watched me, waiting. She must've seen the understanding on my face, because when she spoke next, her voice was soft, the anger gone.

"His name is Michael," she said. "He's a teacher at Sunset Park Elementary. He and I—"

"How long?"

Kara stopped, exhaled. "We met a couple months after you and I split."

I turned away, leaned against the wall. The air in the hallway seemed thin, and my throat felt tight. I couldn't tell if I wanted to scream at her or cry.

Probably both.

"I've talked to an attorney," Kara said. "He's going to contact you directly, unless you have a lawyer you'd like him to—"

"Why didn't you tell me?"

"I'm telling you now."

I laughed. "A little late."

Kara took a deep breath, her shoulders rising and falling. "I didn't expect this to happen, but what I choose to do with my life is none of your business."

"None of my business? I'm still your—"

"We split up, Nick."

I felt the anger burn inside me, but I pushed it back and tried to keep my voice calm. My chest ached at the thought of her with someone else, but I also knew that it was my own damn fault. We were here because of me.

I didn't know what to say.

Kara stood across from me, shifting her weight from one foot to the other, waiting.

"Are you happy?" I asked.

"He's a nice guy, and he's stable."

"Nice and stable," I said. "Sounds like a real whirlwind romance."

The second the words were out of my mouth, I regretted them, but it was too late to take them back. I thought Kara would be mad, but all she did was stare at me.

"I did the whirlwind romance once before," she said. "It had its pretty moments, but this time I'm okay with stable."

I looked away.

"I am sorry, Nick," she said. "I know this wasn't how you thought things would go between us."

I shook my head. "Just stop."

Kara slid her hands back into her pockets and looked down at her feet. For a moment the anger and the hurt faded, and all I saw was the girl I knew all those years ago, the one who'd looked at me in a way no one else had before. The one who'd made me see myself differently.

It'd taken a long time for that look to fade, but eventually it did. The worst part was that I'd let it. Too many arguments, too many harsh words, too much left unsaid.

The weight had been impossible to carry.

"If you're happy," I said, "I'm happy."

I saw the faint bend of a smile on her lips.

"Thank you." She stood straight and adjusted the strap of her purse on her shoulder. "I should probably go. You have company, and I should've called first. I'm sorry to—"

"It's okay."

She motioned to the elevators. "Walk with me?"

I nodded.

Along the way, Kara asked, "Are you really leaving?"

"Looks that way."

"How much trouble are you in?"

"It's not like that," I said. "I've been thinking about a change for a while. This is as good a time as any."

"What did you mean when you said I was involved?"

"You're not," I said. "And I don't want you to worry about anything. I'll handle it, I promise."

Kara was quiet.

"It'll be fine." I smiled. "You have other things to focus on."

I could tell that she didn't believe me, but thankfully she didn't say anything else about it. I didn't want to have to lie to her again.

When we got to the elevators, she pushed the call button, then turned and wrapped her arms around my neck.

"You're a good guy, Nick, despite what you think."

She kissed my cheek, and I closed my eyes and tried to memorize the way her lips felt on my skin. I knew I'd never feel them again, and I wanted to remember.

When the elevator came, Kara stepped inside. She lifted one hand and smiled at me. It was the first time in a long time that I'd seen her look happy.

The elevator doors closed, and I stayed there, listening to the low hum of the motor. Then it stopped and she was gone.

I walked back to my apartment, thinking about what I was going to do next. By the time I opened the door and went inside, I thought I knew.

Abby was sitting on the couch, fully dressed. The table was cleared and the dishes in the sink were washed and drying on the rack.

When she saw me, she stood up. "I'm so sorry, Nick."

I waved her off. "Is there coffee left?"

She told me there was, and I went into the kitchen and poured a cup. Neither of us spoke until I walked back out and sat on the couch.

"Is everything okay?" Abby asked.

"No," I said. "It's not."

"Oh God." Abby put her hands to her mouth. "I'm so stupid. If you don't want to drive me home, I understand. I can call a cab."

I sipped my coffee. "Tell me your plan."

"I don't really have one yet," she said. "I guess Nebraska wouldn't be so bad. I'll have to call around and see if—"

"Not that plan."

Abby frowned. "I don't under—" She stopped talking, and I saw the confusion fade. "You mean Patricia?"

I nodded. "Tell me what we're going to do."

Abby didn't say anything.

All she could do was smile.

PART II

20

Sky View Road ran along the base of the foothills before bending west and snaking its way up to the top of Lookout Mountain. I drove over the loose-gravel road, and Abby navigated from the passenger seat.

"I've only been up here once," she said. "Every time I've seen Daniel, it's been at my house or his office."

"Why's that?"

"He says it's easier to talk at his office, but it's because of her. I'm not welcome up here."

I thought about that and tried to ignore the doubt I felt creeping in. Abby told me Patricia wouldn't make a scene when we showed up, but I wasn't so sure. I didn't know anything about Patricia, but I did know people, and they could be unpredictable when backed into a corner.

I told myself that worrying about it wasn't going to do any good and that it was too late to change my mind. Abby was sure her plan would work, and since I didn't have a better idea, I was along for the ride. Still, the farther up the mountain we went, the more anxious I felt.

Abby must've noticed because she put a hand on my arm and said, "Don't worry, you'll do fine."

I laughed.

"Remember, you're playing a role, that's it." She hesitated. "Just try to be convincing."

"Sounds easy."

"It won't be as hard as you think. Patricia already knows you as the man she hired, so you don't have to convince her you're someone you're not. All you have to do is act the part."

"The part of a killer."

"You can do it."

I wasn't so sure, but I kept that to myself. We'd both find out soon, one way or another.

We drove for a while longer. Then Abby shifted in her seat and pointed to a small white sign hidden behind a line of scrub oak along the side of the road.

"Turn here," she said. "This is the driveway."

I turned at the sign and followed the road through a dense forest of evergreens and cut stone. The road ended at a black iron gate.

"What do I do?" I asked.

"There's a call button," she said. "Push it, and I'll do the talking."

I pulled up to the gate and rolled down the window. There was a keypad with a green service button at the bottom. I pushed it and waited.

A man's voice said, "Can I help you?"

Abby leaned over me. "Abigail Pierce to see Daniel Holloway."

The voice didn't answer, and I heard the speaker click. Abby moved back to her seat, then reached for her shoes on the floorboard and began slipping them on.

"Almost there," she said. "Don't be nervous."

"Are you sure they'll let us in?" I asked. "What if—?"

I didn't get to finish.

There was a low buzz followed by the hum of a motor. Then the gate moved, sliding along hidden rails dug into the road.

"Try to relax," Abby said. "If you act nervous, she'll see it. She's smart, and if she suspects something's wrong or that you're not who she thinks you are, this will all fall apart."

"Great."

"I have faith in you, Nick."

"What if she figures it out?" I asked. "Do we have an exit strategy?"

"An exit strategy?"

"A plan B," I said. "A way out if this doesn't work."

Abby rolled her eyes. "I know what an exit strategy is." She slipped on her last shoe and sat back. "Our plan B is to not fuck up plan A. How's that?"

"About what I expected."

Outside, the motor stopped. The gate was open.

"Okay," Abby said. "Let's get it over with."

I pulled through the gate and started up the long drive-way toward the Holloway house. As I drove, I heard an echo of Victor's voice in my head telling me to be convincing. I couldn't shake it, but I didn't mind.

In a way it actually helped.

———

The Holloway house was built on a raised cliff that overlooked the city. There was a man-made waterfall along the side of the cliff that fed into a slow-rolling stream and ended in a blue pond capped with pink water lilies.

The house was smaller than I'd imagined. The front was almost entirely glass, and the windows cascaded up from the sides to a peak in the center that reflected both the sky above and the city below.

Abby and I parked at the end of a line of cars, then walked along a raised wooden path to a set of stairs leading up to the front door.

"I thought it would be bigger," I said. "This looks small for a billionaire's house."

"He owns others," Abby said. "And it only looks small from the outside."

We stopped at the front door. Abby reached out to ring the bell, but before she could a man in a blue gingham shirt and wire-rimmed glasses opened the door. He looked at me over his glasses, then turned to Abby and smiled a slow, lazy smile.

"Hello, Abigail."

"Hey, Devon." She leaned in and gave him a friendly hug, then said, "I didn't know you were here today."

"We're all here," Devon said. "Mom wanted a family barbecue for Dad. Didn't you get the invitation?"

I saw Abby's eye twitch, but she smiled through it.

"I'm sure it was just lost in the mail."

Devon seemed to understand, and for a minute no one said anything. Then he turned to me and said, "Who's this?"

"This is my new friend, Nick." Abby looped her arm through mine. "Nick, this is Devon, Patricia's oldest son."

I started to reach out to shake his hand, but Devon just nodded and stepped back.

"Well, come on in. Almost everyone is out in the yard." He looked at me. "Would you like a drink, Nick?"

"Scotch if you've got it."

Devon smirked, then turned away. "I'll see what I can find. In the meantime, make yourselves at home."

Once he was gone, Abby leaned in. "That wasn't so tough, right?"

I didn't answer. I was too busy looking around.

The room we were in was bigger than my entire apartment. The floors were polished wood, and the ceiling was vaulted and lined with crystal skylights that lit the room a soft, gentle white. There was a set of French doors along the back wall, surrounded on either side by a series of tall windows that looked out over the yard.

"Shall we find Patricia?" Abby asked. "I'm sure she's lurking around here somewhere."

I nodded, but before I could say anything, Patricia came into the room with Devon and another man I'd never seen before. He was tall with dark hair cut close to his skull, and he stayed a few feet behind Patricia at all times.

"Who is that?"

"That's Travis," Abby said. "He's her assistant."

Patricia stopped in the doorway leading to the kitchen and stared at us both. Then she turned to Travis and whispered something. He nodded and started for the French doors and the barbecue out back.

Devon came over and handed me the drink. Before he walked away, he smirked at me again, except this time I saw what I thought was pity in his eyes.

"Isn't this a surprise?"

Abby and I turned to Patricia. She was wearing white pants and an airy turquoise blouse that hung loose on her thin frame. She had a gold bracelet on her wrist and the same pearl necklace as the night we met.

She stopped several feet from us and folded her arms across her chest. "I didn't know you were coming, Abigail."

"It was a last-minute decision," she said. "Nick wanted to meet the family, so I thought I'd bring him by."

"Is that right?" She looked at me, and I could see her jaw muscles straining under her skin. "Nick, is it?"

I held out my hand. "Nice to meet you."

Patricia stared at my hand until I lowered it. Then she straightened and turned to Abby. "This probably isn't the best time for strangers, considering."

"Nick isn't a stranger," Abby said. "At least not to me. I mean, we just met, but sometimes you just know right away about a person. Besides, I want him to meet Daddy before . . ."

Abby put a hand to her mouth, her voice choked.

If I hadn't known better, I might've been fooled. Instead, I was only impressed.

"Daniel," Patricia said, emphasizing the word, "isn't ready for visitors outside the family. I'm sure we can schedule another time for Nick to meet—"

"Abby!"

The three of us turned toward the back door as three little girls ran into the room carrying neon pink and green Hula-Hoops. They headed straight for Abby.

Abby's face shone. "Hello, triplets."

Patricia looked from the girls to me, and I could see the fear swell in her eyes.

"Girls," she said, waving her hand at them. "Get back outside. Go on, right now."

Abby turned, her voice sweet and comforting. "It's okay. They're just excited to see me."

The girls surrounded Abby, loud and bouncing, waving the Hula-Hoops.

"You have to see what we can do!"

"We didn't know you were coming!"

"Come on, come outside. You have to see!"

Abby laughed, touched my arm. "Nick, this is Haley, Stella, and Ava." She looked at Patricia and smiled. "These little flowers are Patricia's granddaughters."

I felt Patricia tense next to me.

"Girls, this is my new friend, Nick."

One of the girls said, "Hi, Nick." Then she grabbed Abby's arm and pulled her toward the back door. "Come on."

Abby laughed, turned to me. "Will you be okay?"

"I'll be fine."

"Good." She looked from me to Patricia. "You two can get to know each other a little. I won't be long."

Abby leaned in and pressed her lips against mine and held it long enough for it to matter.

One of the girls giggled.

When Abby broke the kiss, she bit her lower lip, then reached up and ran her thumb over mine, shook her head, and whispered, "God, what you do to me."

Then she let go and followed the girls across the room toward the doors leading out to the backyard.

I watched her go, my heart beating heavy.

Once Abby and the girls were gone, Patricia turned on me. When she spoke, it was through clenched teeth.

"Why the fuck is she still alive?"

21

The question took me by surprise, and I wasn't sure what to say. I could feel my hands shaking, so I lifted my glass and took a drink, hoping it would help.

It was like drinking sunlight, and for a moment everything else was forgotten.

"Are you going to explain?" Patricia stepped closer, her voice a whisper. "I paid you to do a job. Why hasn't it been done?"

"You didn't deliver."

"I gave you everything you asked for."

"Not all of it," I said. "The data on the drive was—"

"I gave you everything I had."

"It was incomplete."

Patricia stared at me, then shook her head and looked away. "I don't know what you're talking about."

"Sure you do," I said. "Don't insult me."

"I can't believe this." She pointed toward the front windows and the view of the city stretching out beyond the glass. "There are others who would do this job for the money alone. They wouldn't ask for anything else."

"You're talking about the daughter of one of the richest men in the state," I said. "Not many people out there want that kind of heat."

"We'll see," she said. "Travis found you easily enough. He can find someone else."

"That's not an option."

Patricia opened her mouth to say something, then stopped and shook her head. "I don't understand any of this. That program was shut down years ago. Most of the names we have aren't even up to date. God only knows where half of those people are now."

I stood there, silent.

Patricia shook her head. "This was obviously a mistake. I shouldn't have come to you. Consider yourself fired. I'm calling it off."

"Like I said, it's too late for that."

Patricia waved a hand in the air, dismissing the comment. "Keep the money I paid you, I don't care. Your services are no longer needed."

I watched her as she spoke, and I could tell she was trying to show confidence, but there was a small tremble in her voice that gave her away. Part of me felt sorry for her, but then I thought about Abby and what Victor did to her the night before, all because of Patricia.

After that the feeling faded.

"The people I work for want that information," I said. "Like we agreed."

"And who are these people?" she asked. "Exactly whom do you work for?"

"That's not your concern."

Patricia hugged her arms to her chest, then turned toward the French doors and the windows looking out over the backyard. She didn't say anything, and I wondered if she'd heard me at all.

I started to tell her again, but then she spoke.

"She's evil, you know."

"What?"

"That girl." Patricia nodded toward the back windows. "You obviously have no idea."

I followed her gaze and looked out at Abby standing with the three girls on the patio. The girls were laughing, their neon Hula-Hoops spinning in the sunlight. Abby watched them, her face bright and alive and beautiful.

"She seems like any other girl to me."

Patricia grunted, didn't speak.

I remembered Abby telling me how Patricia hated her from the moment she showed up looking for her father. Now, seeing the way Patricia watched her and hearing the sharpness in her voice, I could see that hatred for myself.

"She's exactly like her mother." Patricia turned to me. "I can see Lillian in her. She was a horrid woman, and her daughter is just as bad."

"I don't care about that," I said. "All I want is the data you agreed to provide. I'll wait while you get it."

Patricia looked at me, her eyebrows arched.

"You want it now?" A hint of a smile formed at the corners of her lips. "Do you honestly think Daniel keeps old records from the lab lying around the house?"

"That's not my problem."

"You do have a one-track mind, don't you?" She turned back to the windows. "I can see why Abby let you into her life. She doesn't like complicated, and I have a feeling that there's not a lot under the surface with you."

I kept quiet.

Patricia sighed and reached for the pearls around her neck. "You don't know anything about her, do you?"

"I know enough."

"Has she told you about her mother?"

"Only that she's dead," I said. "And that she worked as a waitress when she met your husband."

"A waitress?" Patricia laughed. "Lillian must be rolling over in her grave."

"It's not true?"

"Of course it's not true," she said. "Nothing that comes out of that girl's mouth is true." Patricia pointed at me, wagging her finger in the air. "You'd do well to keep that in mind."

"She wasn't a waitress?"

"I can't imagine she was," Patricia said. "When I knew her, she worked with Daniel in the lab. Abby never told you that, did she?"

"She never mentioned it."

"I'm not surprised. Abigail has blinders on when it comes to her mother. Even so, Lillian Pierce wasn't exactly a parent you'd want to brag about." Patricia tapped the side of her head with her fingertip. "She had strange ideas, which was why Daniel let her go and what led to everything that followed."

"Everything that followed?"

"Oh yes," Patricia said. "It was quite the local scandal at the time."

I didn't say anything.

"Ask her about it," Patricia said. "I doubt she'll tell you the truth, but it will be interesting to hear her answer."

I had questions, a lot of them, but the conversation was slipping away from me, and time was running out. I needed to stay focused. Everything else could wait.

"I'm not here to talk about Abby or her mother."

"No, you're not, are you?"

"I want that data."

"Yes, you've made that clear." Patricia shrugged. "Unfortunately, I can't help you."

I finished my drink and set the glass on the table.

"Mrs. Holloway, I don't think I'm explaining the situation clearly. So, I'm going to try again, because I don't want there to be any misunderstanding between us." I stared at her and tried to look intimidating. "You will bring me the information we agreed upon, or—"

"Or what?" Patricia's eyes turned sharp. "What exactly will you do to me?"

I didn't say anything.

"It's you who doesn't fully understand the situation," she said. "If something happens to me, it'll be the first story on the news and on the front page of all the papers. They'll shine a spotlight into every dank little hole in the state to find you—and they will find you, believe me."

"Maybe."

"There's no *maybe* about it." She stepped closer, her eyes never leaving mine. "I know how much people like you hate to come out into the light of day, and I don't believe you're careless enough to bring that kind of attention down on your head, not to mention the people you work for, so I'll ask again: What exactly do you think you're going to do to me if I refuse your request?"

She stopped talking, and I turned toward the French doors and the back windows. I didn't see Abby anywhere, but the three little girls were still on the patio, laughing, the Hula-Hoops spinning joy around them.

I had the most terrible idea.

"You're right," I said. "I won't do anything to you."

Patricia smiled.

"Of course you won't." She straightened herself. "And now that we've made that clear, I think it's time the two of you said your good-byes and—"

"Your granddaughters seem sweet," I said. "Are they really triplets, or did Abby make that up, too?"

Patricia inhaled sharply.

"Which one is the runt?" I asked. "It's Ava, isn't it? She seems so . . ." I let the word hang in the air, hating myself more with each passing second. "Trusting."

I didn't see Patricia coming, and by the time I did it was too late. She slapped me hard across the face, and the sound echoed beneath the tall vaulted ceilings.

When Patricia spoke next, her voice was a low growl.

"How dare you."

"I want the information we agreed upon."

"You come into my house and . . ." Patricia's voice rose as she spoke, but I could hear the panic behind her words. "If you ever threaten my family, my girls—"

"I haven't threatened anyone, Mrs. Holloway."

"How dare you . . ." Her voice cracked, and she put a hand to her mouth, her eyes never leaving me. "What kind of man are you?"

It was a good question, and right then I didn't have an answer. At least not an answer I liked.

"Give me what we asked for and you'll never see me again."

Patricia stepped closer, and it took all my strength to keep from backing up. "I gave you what you asked for."

I frowned, making sure she saw.

"Mrs. Holloway, I'm offering you a second chance to fulfill your end of our agreement."

"Am I supposed to thank you?"

"You're supposed to take advantage." I turned toward the windows and nodded. "Because there won't be another opportunity."

Patricia's lip trembled, and she swallowed hard. "I need to sit down."

I looked around and saw a wooden chair against the wall. I picked it up and carried it over to her. She sat, her legs crossed at the ankle, her shoulders trembling.

She didn't say anything for a long time. When she finally did, her voice was soft and nearly silent.

"I'll need a couple days to search the old records," she said. "I'll have to go to Daniel's lab and see what—"

"Tonight."

She shook her head. "That's impossible. I can't get in there tonight. It would look suspicious."

"Then tomorrow night," I said. "Meet me at Mickey's Pub, the same place as before. Eight o'clock."

Patricia looked up at me, and this time the anger in her eyes was gone. All that was left was sadness and age.

"You're not going to hurt my girls, are you?"

The ache in her voice sank into me.

I wanted to tell her that I wasn't going to hurt anyone and that her family was safe, at least from me. Except that wasn't part of the plan.

In the end, all I did was walk away.

22

Several heads turned as I stepped through the French doors and out onto the patio, but no one spoke to me. A woman in a white shirt carrying an empty tray walked by and asked if I'd like a drink.

I told her I wasn't staying.

There were two tables set up on the grass, both shaded by large baby-blue umbrellas. A few people were sitting on cushioned lawn chairs around the table, but most were wandering around the yard or huddled in smaller groups, eating and talking and laughing.

I didn't see Abby anywhere, and I started to wonder if she'd gone inside. Then I felt a hand on my arm. I looked down and saw one of the little girls staring back up at me, smiling through a scatter of missing teeth.

"Are you Abby's boyfriend?"

"What did she tell you?"

"She said you were just friends, but I think you're her boyfriend."

I crouched down so we were face-to-face. The girl's eyes were wide and blue.

"Have you seen her around?" I asked. "I can't find her anywhere."

The girl looked past me, pointed over my shoulder. "She's talking to Grandpa."

I glanced behind me and saw Abby kneeling next to an old man lying under a blanket on a reclining lawn chair. She had her back to me, so I couldn't see her face.

As I stood up, I noticed Patricia's assistant, Travis, standing a few feet away from Abby. He was staring at her, his hands folded behind his back.

I thanked the little girl, then started walking toward them, but I stopped before I reached the grass. I didn't know what Abby was saying to her father, and I didn't want to interrupt something personal, so I found a spot by the side of the house and waited.

A few minutes later Abby leaned forward, kissed her father on the cheek. I caught a brief glimpse of Daniel Holloway. His skin was thin and blue and hung loose on his face, as if he were melting under the weight of a heavy sun.

I could tell he wasn't going to be around for long.

Abby stood and turned away from her father. Travis moved with her. He caught up, took her elbow, and said something to her as they walked. She didn't respond. From where I stood, her face looked distant and unfocused, almost lost.

Then she saw me, and the darkness around her eyes lifted. Her face became lighter, and when she smiled at me, she shone.

Travis looked up at me and then moved away, leaving her alone. I watched him while I waited for Abby to cross the lawn to where I was standing.

"How'd it go?" she asked. "Did you get it?"

"Tomorrow night," I said. "She's meeting me."

"Tomorrow?" The edge in her voice was sudden and sharp. "They said twenty-four hours."

"She said everything is at Daniel's lab."

"And you believed her?"

I thought about how Patricia had looked when she asked if I was going to hurt her girls, and I nodded.

"Yeah," I said. "I believe her."

I could tell Abby wasn't convinced, but now wasn't the time to talk about it. There were several people standing around the yard, all of them watching us. I felt like I was on display.

"We can talk after we leave," I said. "I saw you with Daniel. Everything okay?"

Abby nodded, looked down.

There was something else there, but I left it alone.

"Then let's get out of here," I said. "I've had enough of this place."

———

We got back in the car and drove down the long gravel driveway, then through the black iron gate and out onto Sky View

Road. I told Abby about my conversation with Patricia. I expected her to be horrified when I told her how I'd threatened Patricia's three granddaughters, but Abby didn't seem to care. She wanted to know about Patricia, how she'd acted, what she'd said.

The excitement in her voice was electric.

"How did she look when you told her?"

"Terrified," I said. "For all she knows I might be the kind of person who would go after her family to get to her. I can't blame her for being scared."

Abby clapped her hands, then held them together in front of her lips. She crossed her legs tight and rocked back and forth, the leather passenger seat moaning under her.

"Are you okay?" I asked.

"I couldn't possibly be better," she said. "You were wonderful, Nick. Simply wonderful."

I didn't understand.

I knew that Abby had a long history with Patricia and that the hatred between them was deep and ran both ways, but still, something about her reaction seemed wrong, and I couldn't quite see it.

"What did her assistant say to you?" I asked.

Abby was staring out the window.

"Who?"

"Big guy, short dark hair."

"Oh, Travis." She shrugged. "Just personal stuff."

"Really?"

"We talk sometimes," she said. "He's not a bad person, not like her."

"He didn't look happy to see me."

Abby laughed to herself. "He's got a thing for me, and he probably sees you as a threat. Nothing to worry about."

I wasn't worried, and I almost told her so, but I decided to let it go. We didn't say anything else, and for a long time we drove in silence.

The giddy energy coming off Abby never faded.

I didn't mind. It was nice to see her happy.

"How did Daniel and your mother meet again?"

"She was a waitress," Abby said. "Why?"

"Patricia mentioned her," I said. "She said I should ask you about her."

"About my mother?"

I nodded.

Abby turned away, and all at once the air in the car seemed to grow thick. I could tell I'd made a mistake bringing it up.

"What did she tell you?"

"Nothing really."

"You're lying."

"I got the impression she didn't like your mother very much, but that's probably because of Daniel."

"That bitch hardly knew my mother, and she has no business talking to you about her." Abby stopped, took a breath. When she spoke again, her voice was strained but calm. "Whatever she told you, it was a lie."

I thought about how Patricia had said the same thing about her, but I kept that to myself. Lillian Pierce was obviously a sensitive subject, and even though I wanted to know more, it wasn't the time to pry. Abby was in a good mood, and after all she'd been through over the past couple days, that was enough for me.

Still, it made me wonder.

———

I drove across town to Jefferson Park and pulled up in front of Abby's house. In the daylight the neighborhood was alive with activity. People were working outside in their yards while kids rode bright-colored bikes along wide sidewalks shaded by towering oak trees.

"Are you going to be okay for a while?"

Abby paused. "You're not coming in?"

"I need to head home."

"But you're coming back?" she asked. "They're going to be here at midnight unless we call. I can't do this without—"

I stopped her, smiled. "I'm coming back."

"You promise?"

"You have my word."

Abby stayed in the car for another minute, watching me. Then she opened her door and said, "I can't thank you enough, Nick—for everything."

"I didn't do any—"

She leaned in, kissed me. Her lips tasted sweet and fresh.

When she pulled away, she took a deep breath, held it, and said, "You saved me."

I felt my throat catch and the back of my neck get hot, but before I could say anything she was out of the car and walking up the path toward her house.

For the first time I allowed myself to notice her.

I watched her wave to one of her neighbors, then take a set of keys from her pocket and unlock the front door. She stopped in the doorway and looked back.

She lifted one hand, then stepped inside and closed the door.

Once she was gone I took my phone from my pocket and dialed Charlie's number. He answered right away.

"About damn time," he said. "Where the hell have you been? How'd it go?"

"I'll fill you in later," I said. "Right now I need another favor. Can you check another name for me?"

"This is pushing it, Nick. I've only got so much goodwill built up down there. Pretty soon someone is going to notice what we're doing and start asking questions."

"Last one," I said. "It's important."

Charlie coughed, said, "What's the name?"

"Lillian Pierce," I said. "Abby's biological mother."

"You're kidding."

"She might've worked for Holloway labs at one time. You could start there."

Charlie grunted, and I heard the sound of a pencil scratching over paper. "And how does she fit in with all of this?"

I glanced out the window toward Abby's house and the closed red door. "That's what I'd like to find out."

23

I stopped at Argo's Liquors on my way home and picked up a fifth of Johnnie Walker and a six-pack. My plan was to lock myself in my apartment and not leave again until I had to go back to Abby's. I needed time alone to clear my head and make sense of everything that'd happened over the past few days.

A couple drinks seemed like a good place to start.

By the time I got back to my apartment, the sun was setting orange behind the mountains, and the air had turned cold. I went in through the lobby and rode the elevator to the third floor, then walked down the hall to my apartment.

I stopped outside my door and adjusted the bag in my arms as I flipped through my keys. My neighbor's television was on, and I could hear the lonely sound of a studio laugh track through the thin walls.

I tried not to think about it.

Once inside I took the bottle of Johnnie Walker from the bag and put the six-pack in the fridge. Abby had done all the dishes that morning, and for the first time in a long time my kitchen was spotless.

I grabbed one of the cups from the dish drainer, then walked out to the living room and sat on the couch. I uncapped the bottle and poured, letting my mind drift.

Of course, it stopped on Kara.

We'd never talked about having kids, at least not seriously, and it was hard to get my head around the idea that she was pregnant, especially when it wasn't mine.

Thinking about her with someone else sat heavy inside me, and I could feel a tight sickness build in the pit of my stomach. I did my best to ignore it, but it was a struggle. Instead, I tried to focus on how happy she'd sounded that morning and the look of joy on her face when she'd told me the news.

In a way it helped.

I reached for my laptop beside the couch and set it on the coffee table. I opened the lid and pulled up a browser and did a quick search for divorce attorneys.

Kara had moved on, and she was happy. It wasn't the way I'd wanted things to turn out, but after all we'd been through together and all she'd put up with from me, I wasn't about to stand in her way now.

After several minutes of looking at legal websites, I felt a small stab of pain form behind my eyes, and the more photos of attorneys I saw, the more the pain grew.

Eventually, I turned away from the screen, refreshed my drink, and then got up and stood in front of the window and stared out at the city lights. I thought about Abby standing in the same spot the night before and saying she'd live here just for the view. At the time I assumed she was trying to make me feel better, but after spending the last twenty-four hours with her I wasn't so sure.

After all she'd been through, she could still find the beauty in the things around her. And while I'd seen enough of the world to know that it wouldn't last, I couldn't help but hope that I was wrong.

I stayed at the window for a while, sipping my drink and going over everything that'd happened over the last couple days. I thought about what Patricia told me about Abby's mother and how there had been some kind of local scandal after she was fired. I'd have to wait until I heard back from Charlie for anything official, but I did have the next best thing. If there had been a scandal, it would've made the news, and if it made the news, I could find it on the Internet.

I finished the last of my drink, then went back to the couch and sat down in front of the laptop. I did a new search—this one for Lillian Pierce, Holloway Industries.

At first I didn't find anything, but then I saw a link to an old report from the *Tribune*. I clicked on it, and it opened an archive page. I scrolled down until I found the headline.

LAB FIRE UNDER INVESTIGATION

Below that, another headline, this one only one word.

ARSON

I pulled up the report and read:

Metro—Dr. Lillian Pierce, a lead researcher at Holloway Industries, is wanted for questioning regarding her possible role in starting a fire that destroyed a large section of the company's research facility.

"Stunned," said Vicky Marshal, the head of Holloway Industries' public relations department. "We are all devastated, not only by the loss of our research, but upon learning that the fire was started by one of our own. I can't begin to express our sadness."

Police say security cameras on the property caught Dr. Pierce entering the building after-hours and dousing a section of the lab in gasoline before starting the blaze. No one was injured in the fire, and Dr. Pierce's location is currently unknown.

"We have issued a warrant for the arrest of Dr. Lillian Pierce," said Detective Caroline Timmel of the Denver Police Department. "She was last seen leaving her home early on the morning of October 5."

According to coworkers, Dr. Pierce became distraught over her future with Holloway Industries and made several threats toward the company. "She said it was her duty to burn it all down," Andrew Lee, a Holloway Industries research assistant, said. "I thought she was joking, but I was wrong."

If you, or anyone you know, have information regarding the location of Dr. Lillian Pierce, please contact the Metro Police Department at . . .

I reached for the bottle and refilled my glass, then leaned back into the cushions. A part of me had thought Patricia lied when she told me about Abby's mother working with Daniel, but the article seemed to back up her story.

I ran through a few more links, all of them reporting the same arson story. I read each of them, hoping for some new insight into why Lillian Pierce did what she did.

Then my phone rang. I answered it as I read.

"Nick?" It was Abby. Her voice was warm and relaxed. "Are you still coming over?"

"Is something wrong?"

"No." She let the word hang in the air, then said, "Things are quiet. I found a bottle of wine in an old box, along with some other stuff."

"Anything interesting?"

"That depends," she said. "Come over and help me finish this bottle of wine."

"Now?" I looked at the clock. "We still have—"

"I don't want to be alone," she said. "Please, Nick."

There was a soft note in her voice that I hadn't heard from a woman in a very long time, and even though I didn't want to leave my apartment, I could see the upside.

"I don't know," I said. "I—"

"I found something I'd like to show you."

"What is it?"

"You have to come over to find out."

I frowned.

"Come on, Nick. Don't say no."

"Okay," I said. "I'll come over."

"Good." I could hear the smile in her voice. "I'll be waiting for you."

We hung up, but I stayed on the couch for a while longer, sipping my drink. I wondered what it was Abby wanted to show me. I had a few ideas, some more appealing than others, and there was only one way to find out.

I finished my drink, then got up and grabbed my jacket and my keys. Before I left, I stopped at the door and looked back at my apartment one last time. Then I walked out into the hall toward whatever came next.

24

I parked in front of Abby's house and walked up the path to her front door. I paused for a second before knocking, then stepped back and waited.

Abby answered the door wearing jeans and a white button-up shirt. Her hair was tied back in a braid, and she had a drink in her hand. When she motioned for me to come inside, the ice clinked delicately against the glass.

"I thought you were drinking wine," I said.

"It didn't last." Abby closed the door behind me, then stepped closer and wrapped her arms around my neck and held me. "I'm glad you're here."

I could smell the alcohol on her, but I didn't mind. She was warm and small, and she felt good in my arms.

After a while I broke the hug.

"What would you like to drink?" Abby asked. "I'm pretty well stocked here, so name it."

"Surprise me."

"I can do that."

I watched her turn the corner into the kitchen. Then I walked into the living room. It looked the same as the night before, and as I stood in the doorway, everything that'd happened came back to me, and I understood why Abby didn't want to be alone.

"I'm happy you're here." Abby's voice sounded thin from the kitchen. "Just so you know, I tried calling the number they gave us last night to tell them what happened."

"You did what?"

"I didn't talk to anyone," Abby said. "I know someone answered because I could hear them breathing, but they didn't say anything."

I walked to the window and looked out through the blinds. The street was quiet, but I stayed at the window for a while longer just to make sure.

"Did you say anything?"

"I told them we needed another day," Abby said. "They just hung up. After that I got scared. That was when I called you."

I closed my eyes, didn't speak.

"Did I screw up?"

"We'll find out at midnight."

"Oh God, I'm sorry."

I told her not to worry, that everything was okay. Then I turned away from the window and looked up at the large painting on the wall, solid black with a vibrant red rectangle stretching across the bottom. It was interesting but also unsettling.

I moved closer.

There was a small card with a handwritten note mounted on the wall next to the painting. I leaned in and read the inscription.

An original for the original.
With joy,
Daniel

"What do you think of it?"

I looked back as Abby came into the living room. She was carrying two glasses and a half-full bottle of scotch. She handed me one of the glasses, filled it, then motioned to the painting.

"Do you like Rothko?"

"It's beautiful," I said. "But I'm not sure why."

Abby laughed. "That's about right." She tilted her head to the side and stared at the painting as if seeing it for the first time. "It's creepy, but it matches the couch."

"Daniel gave it to you?"

"A housewarming gift," she said. "From his private collection."

I looked from the painting to her and then back, convinced I hadn't heard her right. "This is an original?"

"Apparently."

I stepped closer to the painting and read the inscription one more time. "That explains the note. An original painting for his firstborn."

Abby looked down at her glass, took a drink. "Something like that. Daniel can be cryptic."

"Have you had it appraised?"

"I'm never going to sell it."

"Aren't you curious?"

"Not in the least."

I watched her as she backed away and sat on the couch. It was obvious she wasn't interested in discussing the painting, so I decided to let it go.

"Come, sit." She touched the cushion next to her with one finger. "You're making me nervous."

I took one last look at the painting, then crossed the room to the couch and sat next to her. She stared at me for a moment, then reached out and touched my arm.

Her skin was warm and soft on mine.

"Thank you for coming back."

I nodded, took a drink, and tried to settle the bad thoughts pulsing through my head.

"I've been thinking about you since you dropped me off," she said. "I can't stop."

"What have you been thinking?"

Abby looked away. When she spoke again, her voice was loose. "I've been thinking that I owe you an apology."

"For what?"

"For lying to you. I'm not sure why I didn't tell you the truth. I've made such a habit of it that it just came out, and I'm sorry."

"Lied to me about what?"

"My mother."

"What about her?"

Abby held up one finger, then lifted her glass and finished her drink. "Hold on, I'll show you." She set her empty glass on the coffee table, then stood up, bracing herself on the arm of the couch. "I'll be right back."

"Do you need help?"

She ignored me and disappeared down the hall. When she came back, she was carrying a long white envelope. She held it up for me to see, then handed it to me.

"It's all right there."

I flipped the envelope over. There was no writing on the front, but the return address was for the Department of Corrections.

"Go ahead," she said. "Open it."

I hesitated, then opened the flap. There was a single sheet of paper inside, folded in thirds, and I recognized what it was right away.

"A death certificate?"

"My mother's." Abby reached for the bottle and refilled her glass. She spilled a little on the coffee table, but she didn't seem to notice. "From the prison where she died. Notarized and everything."

"I don't understand."

"My mother wasn't a waitress. I lied to you because I was embarrassed, and I didn't want you to know the truth." She reached out and tapped the page in my hand. "This is the truth."

I looked down at the death certificate, silent.

Patricia told me that Abby's mother wasn't a waitress, and I already knew that the police had searched for her regarding the lab fire, but I didn't know that they'd found her or that she'd died in prison.

I decided to act surprised and keep the rest of what I knew a secret. After the way Abby reacted when we left Daniel's house, I figured that would be best.

"How did she die?"

"See for yourself."

I read down the page. "Ovarian cancer?"

Abby nodded.

"How old were you?"

"Fifteen." She reached for the bottle, refilled my drink. "So there you have it. My mother wasn't a cocktail waitress who had a fling with a rich guy. She was something else altogether."

I refolded the death certificate.

"Why was she in prison?"

"DUI."

I looked up at her, but I didn't say anything.

"The thing is, I know she wasn't perfect, but I don't care. She was a good mother and I loved her."

"Of course you did."

"It wasn't always easy," Abby said, waving her glass in the air. She splashed a little onto her hand, and she licked it off. "We were basically homeless a lot of the time, moving from one shitty room to another, but at least we were together. She tried so hard."

I slipped the death certificate back into the envelope and handed it to her. "This doesn't mean anything."

Abby took the envelope, silent.

"It doesn't matter that she wasn't perfect. Look how far you've come." I pointed to the painting. "You found your father, and he was obviously happy to have you in his life."

Abby frowned. "Do you think money means anything?"

"It means you won't starve."

"It's a distraction," she said. "The painting, the money, it's all there to keep you from seeing what's truly important and what really matters."

"And what's that?"

Abby stared at me, her eyes wet and unfocused. "Survival."

"You won't starve if you've got money."

"I'm not talking about food," she said. "I'm talking about not letting those people out there win, not letting them get to you."

"Haven't you already done that?"

Abby set her glass on the coffee table, then inched closer to me. She took my hand in both of hers and leaned in close, her voice soft and slurred.

"I'm talking about taking control, getting that drive from Patricia so they can never touch any of us again." She held up one finger. "That is what is important."

I could smell the alcohol on her breath, and I turned away, squeezing her hands in mine.

"You don't have to worry about that," I said. "After tomorrow it'll all be over. You're safe."

Abby frowned, then reached for her glass. "I'm not that drunk, you know."

"I know," I said. "But you should drink some water, too."

"Do you want a glass of water? I'll get you one."

She tried to stand, but it didn't work.

I smiled. "I'll get it. You stay here."

Abby leaned back on the cushions.

I walked down the hallway and into the kitchen. I found the glasses and filled one with tap water. As I stood at the sink, I glanced out the kitchen window and saw a dark car slow down and pass in front of the house.

I turned off the water and stared out at the street.

The car kept going.

When I went back to the living room, Abby was still on the couch, but her eyes were closed. I set the glass on the coffee table, then put my hand on her shoulder and shook her gently.

"Come on, drink some water."

She mumbled and turned away.

I stood there for a minute. Then I slid my arms under her and picked her up. She was light, and I carried her down the hallway to the bedroom. When I lowered her onto the bed, she made a soft sound and rolled over.

It wasn't exactly the way I thought the night would go.

I walked back to the living room, grabbed the glass of water off the coffee table, and brought it to the bedroom. I set it on her nightstand and was just about to leave when she spoke.

"Nick?"

"Yeah?"

"I'm sorry about all of this," she said. "You're a sweetheart. You deserve better."

I sat on the edge of the bed and brushed the hair from her face. "It'll be over tomorrow. We'll get the flash drive and give it to Victor, and that'll be it."

She nodded. "Okay."

"We might even find out what's on it."

"I already know what's on it."

"You do?"

She nodded, her eyes still closed.

"Okay, tell me."

Abby took a deep breath, exhaled slowly. "Redemption."

I sat there, watching her drift into sleep, and thought about what she'd said. I hoped she was right. I hoped the data on that drive was our way out and that once we had it, all of this would be over for both of us.

When I was sure she was asleep, I got up, took a blanket from the foot of her bed, and covered her.

Abby didn't make a sound.

I went back to the living room and stood at the window and stared out at the street while I finished my drink.

The neighborhood was silent and still.

I took my keys from my pocket, set my empty glass on the coffee table next to Abby's, and then walked out into the darkness, locking her door behind me.

25

The dream is different this time.

I'm in my bed, and again the figure is there, silhouetted in the doorway, watching me. Except this time I know who it is, and when she comes toward me, I'm not afraid.

"Kara?"

She slides over the foot of the bed, snaking her way up until her face is inches from mine.

"How did you get in here? Why are you—?"

Kara presses her lips against mine. I feel her tongue slip between my lips as she pulls the sheets away and climbs on top of me.

"What are you . . . ?"

Kara doesn't answer, and I don't ask again.

I put my hands on her hips and push her down, pressing into her. Kara inhales, sharp, and we stay, neither of us moving. I can feel her breath on my skin, but when I reach out to push her hair away from her face, she sits up and moves against me, her hands flat against my chest.

I close my eyes and arch into her. I run my hands up to her shoulders and work my way down slowly. When I touch her breasts, I stop.

Something is wrong, and I open my eyes.

Kara's left breast is shriveled and rotted black.

I make a noise deep in my throat and pull away. When I do, the skin of her breast slides off like a wet sheath in my hand.

I cry out and try to sit up, but Kara pushes me down, her face hidden behind a veil of hair. I reach for her shoulders and try to move her, but she squeezes her legs tight and grinds against me, pushing me deeper into the mattress.

I feel myself sinking as she moves faster, her breath pulsing in and out in short guttural moans. I try to force her off of me, but it's too late. I can feel myself slipping into a beautiful, calm darkness, and the farther down I go, the less I want to fight.

Drowning.

I look up and watch her from under the surface. Except this time it's not Kara.

It's Abby.

The left side of her chest is open, oozing wet and black, dripping down her stomach, covering us both.

I want to wake up.

I close my eyes and try to will myself awake, but then I feel her hands tighten on my throat, and I can't breathe.

I open my eyes.

Abby is leaning over me, smiling, showing rows of tiny sharp teeth. She stares down at me, her head tilted to the side, birdlike. Then she leans in and I feel her teeth close on my cheek, digging into my flesh.

The pain is everywhere, and I scream.

Abby's hand tightens on my throat, cutting off the air. I can feel the blood running down the side of my face, soaking into the sheets, and the desperate lapping of her tongue, wet and cold against my skin.

My vision fades and the darkness creeps in.

I don't fight it.

When Abby pulls back, her mouth is ringed red.

She runs her tongue over her teeth and then presses her hands against my chest. I feel her entire body shudder as she squeezes her legs tight around me.

Then she turns her face to the sky and roars.

———

I was jolted awake.

I felt several hands on me, pulling me up and out of bed, dragging me across the floor. I tried to fight, tried to pull away, but I was outnumbered, and I couldn't get my legs under me.

They carried me into the living room. Victor was standing next to the kitchen table. He took one of the chairs and slid it across the floor to the middle of the room, then took a plastic zip tie from his pocket.

"No," I said. "Wait."

I fought, but they pushed me down onto the chair. For a second I managed to break their grip, and I hit one of them across the face with an elbow. The sound he made gave me hope, but it didn't last.

Someone hit me in the center of the chest, and everything inside of me twisted and cramped. I dropped to one knee, struggling to breathe.

They didn't give me a chance.

The men lifted me into the chair and bent my arms behind my back. Victor handed one of them the zip tie, and he wrapped it around my wrists, securing it tight.

I knew I should be scared, but I wasn't.

I was furious.

The cramping in my chest started to fade, and my breath came back a little more. I wanted to fight, but I couldn't move. I screamed at them to let me go, but then Victor nodded, and one of the men behind me grabbed my hair and jerked my head back hard. He pushed a leather strap into my mouth, securing it around my head.

Then he leaned in and whispered, "You're going to want to bite down."

The words settled cold inside me, and I looked up at Victor, who stepped closer and crouched in front of me.

"Hello, Nick."

I closed my eyes and slowed my breathing and tried to stay calm.

It worked for a moment, but it didn't last.

"I'd hoped after our last talk that you understood what was expected of you." Victor bit the insides of his cheeks. "I thought I'd made myself clear when I said midnight, but I realize now that I was too subtle."

I tried to speak, tried to explain everything to him, but my words were broken and muffled by the strap.

Victor waited until I stopped talking, then asked, "Do you have the drive?"

I didn't want to say no, not without explaining, so I didn't say anything.

"Nick?" Victor's voice was calm but cold. "It's an easy question. Do you have the drive? Yes or no?"

I turned to face him, but I still didn't answer.

Victor nodded to one of the men behind me.

Someone reached down and grabbed my hands. I felt him straighten the middle finger on my left hand and press the back of my knuckle against the leg of the chair.

I knew what was coming.

I tried to tell them to stop, but they didn't, and Victor watched, silent.

I bit down on the leather strap as the man behind me held my hand against the leg of the chair and pushed the top of my finger back hard, snapping the bone at the knuckle.

The pain was shocking.

When I opened my eyes, the room was spinning, and I had to hold my breath to keep from throwing up.

Victor's eyes never left mine.

"This seems bad, doesn't it?" He studied me. "Unfortunately, I need an answer. The good news is that I'm only going to ask the question nine more times. After that?" He paused. "Well, we'll just have to see."

My head was down, resting on my chest.

"Are you still with us, Nick?"

I looked up at him, the room still spinning around me, and started repeating the same word over and over.

"Tonight."

It sounded muffled and weak behind the leather strap, but I didn't stop until Victor looked past me and nodded.

I felt a rush of panic and adrenaline rage through me, and I fought hard, twisting in the chair, screaming. It wasn't until someone loosened the leather strap that I started to calm down.

Once the strap was off, I started talking. I told them everything. When I finished, Victor stood up and paced the room. I could see his lips moving, but there was no sound.

All I could do was wait.

"Mr. Ellis will stay with you until the time comes to meet the woman." He stopped pacing and faced me. "We will escort you to her, and then you will deliver the new drive directly to me. Is that understood?"

I nodded.

"There will be consequences if you fail."

"I won't fail."

Victor stared at me for a moment longer, then said, "Cut him loose."

I felt a cold blade slide under the zip tie, followed by a quick movement, and then I was free. I held my hand in my lap and looked down at my twisted finger.

My stomach lurched, and I turned away.

Victor started for the door, and everyone but Ellis followed. Before he walked out, he stopped and turned back.

"Don't make me regret this charity, Nick. My patience is truly at an end."

"I'll get it," I said.

And this time I meant it.

26

I filled a plastic bag with ice, then took a roll of duct tape from the drawer in the kitchen and went into the bathroom. Ellis stood by the front door, his hands folded in front of him, watching me.

I ignored him.

There was an expired bottle of Percocet in the medicine cabinet, and I tapped the last three pills out into my hand. I swallowed them one at a time, hoping they were still good, and then I leaned against the sink and stared at my reflection in the mirror.

I'd seen better days.

I looked down at my twisted finger, then opened the bag of ice and slipped my hand inside. I tore away three strips of duct tape with my teeth while I was waiting for my finger to go numb, and I lined them up along the edge of the sink.

When I felt ready, I reached for the hand towel on the rack and wrapped it around my broken finger. Then I took a deep breath and pulled, straightening my finger with one quick, hard movement.

The room flashed, and I eased myself down, sitting on the edge of the bathtub and cradling my broken finger in the towel. My eyes were watering, and my stomach was rolling. I kept my eyes closed and focused on my breathing, trying to not throw up.

A minute later Ellis came around the corner and stood in the doorway.

I looked up at him. "Fuck off."

He stood there for a moment longer, then turned away.

Once he was gone I unwrapped my finger. It was straight enough, but the knuckle was off center and turned slightly toward my thumb. I thought about trying again but decided once was enough.

I pulled the strips of tape from the sink one by one and taped my middle finger to my ring finger. Then I leaned forward, elbows on knees, and waited. My head felt light, but that was a good sign. It meant the Percocet was kicking in. I told myself that I should eat, but the thought of food made my throat clench.

All I wanted to do was sleep.

I reached out for the sink and used it to steady myself as I stood. Once I had my feet under me, I walked slowly out of the bathroom. Ellis was standing by the window in the living room, but I ignored him and inched along the hallway toward my bedroom.

The last few feet were the hardest.

Eventually, I made it, and I eased myself back onto the mattress and stared up at the ceiling, waiting for the room to stop spinning. I tried to keep my mind focused on Patricia and our meeting later that night, but I kept going back to all the things that could go wrong, making it hard to relax.

After a while I felt myself start to fade.

I didn't fight it.

———

"Get up."

I opened my eyes. The room was dark, and I could see the shadow of Ellis standing over me. I lifted my head and looked at the clock on the bedside table. The display flashed 12:00.

"What time is it?"

"Time to go," Ellis said. "Get dressed. You have five minutes."

He turned and walked out.

I gathered my strength, then sat up on the edge of the bed, waiting for my head to clear. I could feel my broken finger pulsing under the tape, and I cursed myself for not saving one of the painkillers.

In the other room Ellis shouted, "Four minutes."

"Yeah, fuck you," I said, keeping my voice quiet.

I looked around the room for my clothes, then stood up and got dressed. My throat was rough and dry, and there was a sharp pain screaming at me from behind my eyes. I tried to ignore it.

When I walked out of the bedroom, I went straight to the kitchen. I poured myself a glass of water, finished it, then poured another. When it was empty, I set the glass in the sink and grabbed my cell phone from the charger on the counter. There were three missed calls, all from Charlie.

I started to call him back, but Ellis stopped me.

"No calls."

I didn't argue.

Instead, I grabbed my coat off the back of the couch and headed for the door.

Ellis followed me into the hallway. We rode the elevator to the lobby, then walked out the front door to the street. The black SUV was parked at the curb, blanketed in a thick evening fog.

Ellis pointed to the passenger door. "You're in front."

I reached for the door handle and looked inside. Victor was in back behind the driver's seat. David was next to him. Neither said a word.

I got in and watched Ellis walk around to the driver's side. He started the engine, put the car in gear, and pulled out onto the street. No one said anything until we stopped half a block from Mickey's Pub.

"Keep it short," Victor said. "Get the drive and get out. We'll be waiting here to pick you up."

I nodded.

Victor checked his watch, then pointed to the door. I started to get out, but then I felt his hand close on my shoulder, and I looked back.

"No surprises, Nick."

"Don't worry," I said. "There won't be."

———

The fog outside was wet and thick, and I closed my coat tight around my chest as I walked down the block toward Mickey's. There was a silver Mercedes parked out front, and Patricia's driver, Travis, was sitting behind the wheel, watching me.

I pretended I didn't see him and went inside.

For a Monday, Mickey's was busy. There were several people at the bar, and most of the tables were taken. Mickey was talking to customers and making drinks. He didn't see me come in.

I stood in the doorway and scanned the room for Patricia. I didn't see her right away, so I made my way up to the bar and waited for Mickey to see me. When he did, he gave me a half salute, then turned back to the line of glasses in front of him.

"Be with you in a sec, Nick."

I sat on the closest stool and looked around at the crowd. Most of the people in the bar were younger—college students—gathered around the tables in loud groups. I listened to them talk while I waited for Mickey to work his way down the bar to me, but I got bored fast, and I stopped paying attention.

A minute later someone stepped up and set a half-empty martini glass on the bar beside me. I looked over and saw Patricia draping her coat over the stool next to mine.

She sat down and said, "Here we are again."

Before I could say anything, Mickey came up and dropped two napkins on the bar in front of us. He had a rocks glass in his hand, and he set it in front of me, then reached for the Macallan bottle on the shelf.

I watched as he poured the drink. When I looked up at him, he raised his eyebrows and nodded toward Patricia.

I shook my head.

"If you two need anything, just yell." He put the bottle back on the shelf. "I'll be right over here."

He turned away, leaving us alone.

For a moment neither of us spoke. Then Patricia lifted her glass and held it out in front of her, waiting.

"Are we drinking to something?" I asked.

"Of course," Patricia said. "To this being the last time we ever see each other."

I touched my glass to hers. "One can only hope."

27

W e might as well get on to business." Patricia reached for her coat on the bar stool and took a silver flash drive from one of the pockets. She held it out to me and said, "I believe this is what you're after."

"Is this everything?"

She nodded. "And just so we're clear, now that I've delivered on my end I expect you to deliver on yours. There's still a job to be done."

I pocketed the flash drive.

"That's not going to happen."

Patricia shook her head. "Why am I not surprised?" She lifted her glass, took a drink. "When I saw you two together, I knew she had her claws in you."

I ignored the comment, said, "Can I ask you something?"

"If you'd like."

"Why do you hate her?"

"Abigail?"

"Is it the money? Was that why you hired me?"

"What money is that?"

"Her inheritance."

"Inheritance?" Patricia turned, her face bright. "Did she tell you Daniel was leaving her money?"

I opened my mouth to say something, then stopped.

Patricia laughed. "That girl, she's unbelievable."

"It's not true?"

"Of course it's not true," she said. "I'm Daniel's wife and his sole beneficiary. Everything comes to me."

I couldn't understand why Abby would lie to me about her inheritance. It didn't make sense, but it did make me wonder what else she wasn't telling the truth about.

"If it wasn't money, then why hire me?"

"How can you ask me that?" Patricia's voice turned cold. "You've seen my husband. You've seen what she did to him."

"You blame her for his stroke?"

"Of course I do," she said. "His illness is a direct result of her coming back."

"That seems unfair."

"Daniel isn't a young man," Patricia said. "He'd never admit it, especially after she showed up, but facing those memories was hard on him. The stress was too much to handle. So yes, I blame her completely."

"What memories?" I asked. "He never knew her."

"Project Aeon," Patricia said. "Those memories never left him."

I stared at her, silent.

"You have no idea what I'm talking about, do you?" She frowned. "Do you know what I just gave you?"

I started to answer, but I didn't know what to say.

"My Lord." Patricia set her glass on the bar. "There are people all over the world who would kill to get their hands on the information in that flash drive, and it winds up in your pocket." She smiled, looked away. "How fitting."

"What is it?"

"It's a lifetime of work," she said. "Daniel's mostly, but Lillian's, too."

"Abby's mother?"

"Project Aeon was as much Lillian's passion as it was Daniel's. He was the lead of course, but Lillian worked with him every step of the way." Patricia stopped talking, smiled. "It was their baby, so to speak."

"Were you part of it?"

"God, no." She shook her head. "My first husband was one of Daniel's early backers before he passed, which was how we met. I didn't learn about Project Aeon until much later, long after Daniel shut it down."

I didn't say anything else right away. I had too many questions, and I wasn't sure where to start. Eventually, I decided to start at the beginning.

"What was this project?"

Patricia reached for her glass, sipped. "They were looking for a way to cheat death."

I stared at her, silent.

She set her glass on the bar, then touched the edge of her mouth with her thumb and looked at it. "That's a simplistic explanation, but it holds true."

"I don't understand."

Patricia sighed. "Aeon was a black project. It was run by a subgroup outside the company and subsidized by a group of civilian and military leaders. Their goal was to develop ways to prolong the human lifespan."

"A lot of companies are trying to do that."

"Yes, but in this case there were no restrictions. They wanted results, and they weren't concerned with the moral implications of their methods."

"Their methods?"

"They didn't want to wait for approval to test their findings on human test subjects." Patricia shrugged. "So they didn't."

I thought about the flash drive in my pocket, then said, "Did it work? Did they succeed?"

"They did," Patricia said. "In a way."

"What does that mean?"

Patricia looked at me. "Are you sure you want to hear this? I was under the impression that you were nothing but a middleman. You can't possibly be interested."

"I'd like to know what I'm involved in."

Patricia smiled. "That's the smartest thing I've heard you say yet." She finished her drink, then held up the empty glass for Mickey to see. "Yes, it worked. There were a few minor complications, but for all intents and purposes Project Aeon was a success."

"You're telling me Daniel and Lillian figured out a way to cheat death?"

"You can't actually cheat death," Patricia said. "But they did find a way to put it off for quite a while."

"How?"

"If you're asking how they did it, I'm not the person to ask," she said. "Daniel was the expert, not me. He never told me any of this until after we were married, and by then the project had been shut down for years."

"Then how do you—?"

"He tried to explain it to me once or twice, but only to keep it straight in his head. I'm afraid it was always a bit over mine." She ran a finger along the rim of her empty glass. "If he were here, he'd be able to answer all your questions much better than I can, but that's no longer a possibility."

I started to say more, but then Mickey came up with Patricia's drink, and I stopped talking.

"One vodka martini." He set the drink in front of her, then looked at me. "You want another, Nick?"

I told him I didn't.

Mickey nodded, walked away.

Patricia took the olive from her drink. "They seem to know you."

"I've been here before."

Patricia put the olive in her mouth, didn't speak.

"They figured out a way to cheat death, but you—"

"Ah." She held up one finger. "Postpone death."

"Okay," I said. "But you don't know how they did it."

"DNA modification in utero." Patricia sipped her drink, winced. "But like I said, I'm not an expert."

"What kind of modification?"

"They were able to filter out genetic disorders," she said. "Heart disease, cancer, diabetes, the usual suspects. But then they took it further and found ways to strengthen internal organs, boost the immune system, and slow cellular decay. Basically, they learned how to slow, and in some cases even stop, the negative effects of aging on the human body before the subject was even born."

"That's incredible."

"There were fifty-one healthy babies born into Project Aeon before Daniel closed it down."

"And they were all—"

"Enhanced." Patricia nodded. "That's right."

One of the girls at the next table screamed, then laughed loud. The sound pulled me back, reminding me where I was and what I was there to do.

Still, I had more questions.

"The children were normal?"

"Perfectly normal," Patricia said. "Except that injuries healed quicker for them than other kids, and they rarely, if ever, got sick. Barring accidents or suicide, every one of them should live long, healthy lives well into their hundreds, if not longer."

I stared at her, silent.

Patricia smiled. "Daniel was a brilliant man."

"So what happened?"

"With the children?"

"With the project," I said. "Why did he close it down? Was it because of Lillian and the fire?"

Patricia looked up at me. "You know about the fire?"

"I did my research."

"Impressive," she said. "Did you know that Lillian was furious when she found out Daniel was ending the program? I'll always believe she started the fire to hurt him."

"I don't understand why he stopped. If it was such a success, why end it?"

"He never told me the reason behind his decision, and I never asked," she said. "I believe he was under pressure from the military to find a solution to the complications or to turn his research over to them and—"

"What were the complications?"

Patricia turned to face me. "Is that important?"

"I'd like to know."

She took a drink, said, "All the embryos were cultivated in the lab and then transferred back to the mother. A fairly simple procedure, but in nearly half the cases the mother would miscarry, always at around six to eight weeks."

"Why?"

"No one knew," she said. "Eventually they were able to tie it to the development of the Y chromosome, but they were never able to solve the problem."

"The Y chromosome?" I thought about it. "Boys."

Patricia nodded. "That seemed to be the catalyst, because out of all the children born into Project Aeon, not a single one was male."

28

Patricia looked at her watch, then lifted her glass. "As fun as this has been, I think we're done here."

"Why did you tell me all of this?"

Patricia seemed to think about it for a moment. Then she shrugged and said, "The shadow of that project has been hanging over my family for a long time. Now I'm washing my hands of the entire thing."

"That's it?"

"And because you asked." She finished the last of her martini and set the empty glass on the bar. "I also thought you should know what it was that you were delivering."

"I still don't have a clue."

"Now, that's a shame," Patricia said. "Are you unable to connect the dots?"

I frowned. "You said it was Daniel's work with Project Aeon, but I thought all of that was destroyed in the fire."

"Nearly all of it, that's true."

"Then no, I still don't understand." I took the flash drive out of my pocket and held it up in the dim light. "If it's not his research, then what is it?"

"It's the project itself."

I stared at her. "I don't—"

"Project Aeon was more than the research. It was a team of scientists and volunteers who dedicated years to the project." She pointed to the drive. "That is what you're delivering."

"A list of the people involved?"

"From the top down," she said. "Everyone from Daniel and the financial backers down to the children born into the project and their families."

I stared at the drive. "Names?"

"Names, titles, contact information." She smiled. "I left the children off last time, thinking I could protect their privacy, but I was wrong. The people you work for obviously believe they're important."

"But why?"

"That's a good question." Patricia took her coat off the bar stool and folded it in her lap as she spoke. "Most of the people on that list have moved on. They're scattered all around the world. So why would someone want to know their names and how to find them?"

I thought about it and was about to say something else when the door opened and Ellis came inside. He scanned the crowd until he saw me, then walked to one of the front tables and sat down.

"Something wrong?" Patricia asked.

"No," I lied. "Just trying to make sense out of this."

Patricia slid off the bar stool and stood up. "Whatever their reason for wanting that information, I'm washing my hands of it all. I suggest you do the same."

"That's what I've been trying to do." I held up my glass and motioned to Mickey. "But I'm stuck."

"Then I'll give you a little advice." Patricia slipped into her coat and began fastening the buttons over her chest, but her eyes never left mine. "Don't tell the people you work for what we discussed tonight. Don't let them know that you're aware of what's on that drive."

"Why not?"

Patricia opened her mouth to speak, but before she could, Mickey walked up and refilled my glass.

"Are you leaving us?" he asked. "It's early."

"No," Patricia said. "It's actually very late." She took a fold of bills out of her pocket, peeled two off the top, and set them on the bar. "The drinks are on me tonight."

Mickey turned to me. "Aren't you the lucky man?"

I didn't say anything, and Patricia held out her hand. "I wish you the best, Mr. White, and I'm truly sorry you became mixed up in all of this."

I heard what she said, but it took a minute before I understood.

"You know my name?"

Patricia smiled. "You don't think I'd let someone come into my house and threaten me and my family without finding out all I could about them, do you?"

I stared at her, silent.

"I understand now what happened, and I sympathize with the position you find yourself in. I realize that you're not a threat, but I do believe the people you're associated with are." She let go of my hand and stepped away. "Please let them know that our dealings are at an end. Good-bye, Nick."

Patricia turned, and I watched her walk toward the door. She didn't look at Ellis as she left, but I saw his eyes follow her until she was gone.

I picked up my glass and drank.

"What was that all about?" Mickey asked.

I shook my head, then glanced over at Ellis. In a few minutes I was going to hand the flash drive off to Victor, and I wondered what would happen once I did.

With no further use for me, why keep me alive?

"Nick?"

I looked up at Mickey.

"You okay?" he asked. "You seem off."

I glanced back at Ellis. One of the waitresses was standing next to him, talking.

"I need to ask a favor," I said. "Can you help me?"

"Name it."

"Got a pen?"

Mickey took a black Sharpie from his pocket and handed it to me. I reached for a clean napkin and wrote Kara's phone number on the back.

"If you don't hear from me in the next forty-eight hours, I want you to call this number and talk to Kara."

Mickey frowned. "I don't think I like this."

"I want you to tell her I'm sorry."

"What's going on, Nick?"

I shook my head, looked back at Ellis.

The waitress was gone, and he was staring at me.

"I can't tell you now," I said. "I just need you to do this for me."

"If you're in trouble, I can—"

"Please," I cut him off. "This is important."

Mickey was quiet for a moment. Then he took the napkin and pocketed it. "All right, but if you're in trouble—"

"Just remember, forty-eight hours."

Mickey nodded. "Is there anything else I can do?"

"Yeah," I said, standing up. "You can wish me luck."

I headed for the door, and Ellis followed.

Once outside I felt his hand on my arm, leading me up the street.

I pulled away.

Ellis backed off, and we walked through the fog toward the SUV. I did my best to stay calm, but my heart was beating in my throat, and my chest ached.

When we got to the SUV, Ellis stepped in front of me and opened the passenger-side door. Victor and David were in the back. Victor waited until Ellis and I were inside. Then he said, "Let's go."

Ellis pulled away from the curb and we drove.

We were a block away from Mickey's when Victor sat up and held his hand out, palm up.

I took the flash drive from my pocket. "She said it's all there."

Victor hesitated. "Did she tell you what it was?"

His tone was icy, and I swallowed hard, remembering Patricia's warning.

"I didn't ask."

My voice must've sounded steadier than I thought, because Victor didn't say anything else. He handed the drive to David, who opened his laptop.

I turned and watched the streetlights roll quietly through the fog outside my window.

The sound of David typing made it hard to concentrate. After a while I stopped trying and started paying attention to where we were going.

Eventually, we left downtown and drove into the warehouse district.

Deserted and dark.

I didn't want to read anything into it, but that was hard to do. At night the warehouse district was empty, the buildings were dark, and there was no one around.

No witnesses.

David stopped typing. I looked back. Victor whispered something to David that I couldn't quite hear. David nodded and closed the laptop.

Victor touched Ellis on the shoulder. "Pull over up here."

A thin line of sweat ran down the middle of my back, sending a wave of chills through me as the SUV slowed and stopped next to a line of blue Dumpsters and an alley leading off into fog and shadow.

"This is your stop, Nick," Victor said. "Get out."

I paused, feeling everyone watching me. Then I reached for the handle and opened the door. The overhead light came on bright, and it burned my eyes.

"She told me it was all there," I said. "If she—"

"Out," Victor said. "Now."

I stepped out into the cold and closed the door behind me. I thought about running, but then Victor's window slid down, and I made myself stay.

"You're free to go," he said. "But I would suggest taking that trip you've been planning. If we see you again, things will end differently."

A wave of relief passed over me, but it didn't last.

"What about Abby?"

"Not your concern."

"We had a deal," I said. "We get you the drive, and you let us go. Both of us."

Victor stared at me, a deep line forming between his eyebrows. "If you're unhappy with how things have turned out, we can always—"

"We had a deal," I said. "I need to know she's safe."

Victor stared at me for a moment longer, and I felt everything inside me go cold.

"She's safe," he said. "Now go home, Nick. Today has been a good day for you. Enjoy it."

Victor's window slid up, and the SUV pulled away.

I stood on the side of the road and watched until the red taillights faded away into the fog and I was alone.

29

I called Abby as I walked home. She answered right away, and when I told her what had happened, she squealed.

The sound filled me, and I couldn't help but smile.

"Then it's over?" she asked. "It's really over?"

I told her it was.

"Oh my God, Nick."

"I can't believe it worked," I said. "But we did it."

"No, you did it." I could hear the smile in her voice. "I don't know what to say or how to thank you."

I felt my face go flush, and even in the cold night air, my cheeks burned. "You don't have to thank me."

"Where are you?"

I stopped on the corner and read the street names, then said, "They dropped me in the warehouse district. I'm walking home, but I've still got a ways to go."

"Nick, I don't know what to say."

"You don't have to say anything."

"What are you going to do now?"

"I'm going to go home, take a shower, and then have a doctor look at my finger," I said. "After that—"

"Your finger?"

"Don't worry about it," I said. "It's fine."

I could tell she wanted to ask more, but I didn't want to upset her, so I changed the subject.

"You should still be careful," I said. "Patricia came after you once. She could try again."

"I'm not worried about her," Abby said. "Right now I feel like the weight of the world has been lifted. I want to celebrate. What are you doing tonight?"

"I need to see my father," I said. "I'm sure he wants to know what's happening."

"I bet he'll be happy you're not leaving anymore."

I didn't say anything.

"You're not still leaving, are you?" Abby asked.

"I haven't decided."

This time it was Abby's turn to be quiet.

I let the silence grow, then swallowed hard and said, "You could come with me."

"Nick." Her voice was soft. "You barely know me."

"I'll get to know you," I said. "And I'm not saying we go with any kind of expectations, only that we get the hell out of here for a little while, as friends."

Abby hesitated. "Can I think about it?"

"Yeah," I said. "I need to wrap up some loose ends around here, anyway. I'm not going anywhere for a while."

Silence.

"Are you okay?" I asked. "I hope I didn't—"

"I'm fine," she said. "No, I'm great, actually. Will you have dinner with me this weekend?"

"What?"

"As a thank-you," she said. "Not a very good one, considering everything you've done for me, but I'd like to take you out."

"Like on a date?"

Abby laughed. "Is that too forward? You did just ask me to run away with you, you know."

"You're right," I said. "I did."

"So, it's a date?"

I thought about it, but not for too long.

"Yeah, it's a date."

———

Abby and I talked while I walked the rest of the way home. By the time we hung up, I no longer noticed the cold.

When I got to my building, I stopped at the front door, then changed my mind and kept walking down the street to where I'd parked. There was a government-green parking ticket under the windshield. I pulled the ticket out, crumpled it, then took the keys from my pocket and climbed in.

Before I started the engine, I leaned back in the seat and closed my eyes, letting everything sink in. Somehow I'd come out of a bad situation better off than when I went in, and I couldn't help but smile.

My luck had changed.

I started the engine and drove. I'd just reached the high-way when my phone rang. I looked down at the name on the ID, then put the phone to my ear.

"I was just on my way to see you," I said. "You're still up?"

"Of course I'm still up," Charlie said. "Where are you? Is everything okay?"

I could tell he was trying to sound tough, but his voice was tense and worried.

"Everything's fine, Pop," I said. "I'll be there in about twenty minutes. I've got a lot to tell you."

"I've got a lot to tell you, too," he said. "I looked into the name you gave me, Lillian Pierce. She's got quite a history."

"Yeah, I know."

"Did you know she was some kind of genius?" Charlie asked. "Graduated from Stanford when she was nineteen, top of her class. Then went on to Harvard and got her doctorate a few years later."

"I didn't know that."

"It's true," Charlie said. "And you were right about her working at Holloway Industries. She started there right out of school and stayed for a few years until she apparently had some kind of breakdown."

"The fire."

Charlie paused. "You know about it?"

"Only a little."

"Well, you're right, there was a fire," he said. "She disappeared after that. Gone for about a decade. Then six years ago she was arrested for a DUI. They ran her name and prints through the system, and that was it. They got her."

"After ten years?"

"Everyone gets sloppy," Charlie said. "I don't care how careful they are, eventually they slip up and it all comes apart."

"Still, ten years."

I heard the sound of pages being turned. Then Charlie said, "She was convicted of arson and endangerment, along with a list of evasion charges. She went inside and died during her first year. Cancer of some sort."

"Ovarian."

Charlie paused. "How much of this did you know?"

"I knew about the fire and that she died in prison."

"How?"

"Abby told me about the cancer," I said. "She showed me the death certificate."

"That reminds me," he said. "Abigail Pierce. I finally got the rest of her information back, for what it's worth. There's not much there."

"What information?"

"The last of her background check," he said. "It's mostly foster care records. She wasn't there long enough to build much of a file. I was hoping for her medical records to see about the paternity test, but we're still having trouble with those."

"What kind of trouble?"

"Someone screwed up," Charlie said. "They sent them to us twice, and both times they've been incomplete."

"What do you mean *incomplete*?"

"There's nothing there," he said. "Couple routine exams, and that's it."

"What does that mean?"

"It means that someone made a mistake and lost her medical records." Charlie laughed. "Either that or she's never been sick a day in her life."

The words seemed to hang in the air.

I felt myself sinking, and I stared out at the dark road ahead, silent.

"You still there?"

"I'm . . ." My voice cracked and my throat tightened. "I've got to go, Pop. I'll call you in a little while."

"I thought you were coming over."

"Later," I said. "There's something I need to do."

Charlie paused. "What's going on?"

I wanted to tell him everything was fine, but the words wouldn't come. Instead, I hung up and dropped the phone on the passenger seat, then pulled over and turned around, heading back toward the city and Jefferson Park.

I drove in silence, and the road rolled black in front of me.

30

Abby's lights were on when I arrived. I saw her shadow through the window as I walked up the path, and when I got to the porch I could hear her singing along to the radio.

I knocked, waited.

The music stopped, and I heard footsteps inside. Then Abby opened the door just enough to see out. When she saw me, she pulled the door open and smiled.

"You're here."

I stared at her, silent.

"What's wrong?"

"You and I have to talk," I said. "Can I come in?"

She hesitated, then stepped back, letting me pass. Once I was inside, she closed the door and slid the bolt into place, then turned on me.

"You said this was over."

"I thought it was."

"What happened?"

"Maybe nothing," I said. "But I wanted to talk to you and make sure."

Abby leaned back against the closed door. "You're starting to scare me, Nick. What's going on?"

"Can we sit down?"

"Just tell me."

I stared at her, unsure where to start. "Have you ever heard of Project Aeon?"

Abby's eye twitched, and I could tell by the way she looked at me that I'd found a sensitive spot.

"How do you know about that?"

"Did your mother ever tell you what she was—?"

"Patricia."

"What?"

"She told you, didn't she? About my mother." Abby folded her arms over her chest. "What did she say to you?"

"Everything."

Abby laughed, but there was no humor in it. "I seriously doubt that."

"That's why we need to talk." I motioned toward the living room. "Can we sit down? I don't know how much time we have, and I don't want to waste it."

Abby pushed away from the door and angled past me, heading for the living room. I followed her, and we both sat on the red couch.

"Okay," she said. "Now tell me."

"We might have a problem."

"No." Abby shook her head. "We made a deal. We got them what they wanted. They agreed—"

"It's not that."

"Then what are you talking about?"

"Patricia told me what was on the flash drive," I said. "She said it was some kind of master list of everyone who was directly involved with Project Aeon."

"What does that have to do with me?" Abby asked. "That was my mother and Daniel, not me."

"Did she ever tell you what they were working on?"

"Why would she?" Abby asked. "I was just a kid. Even if she had told me, it was science stuff. I didn't care."

I nodded, looked away.

"What is this about, Nick?"

"I think you're still in danger."

"Why?"

"Because I think your name is on that master list."

———

I went over everything Patricia told me about Abby's mother and Project Aeon. When I finished, Abby leaned back on the cushions and stared out at nothing for a long time.

I asked her if she was okay.

"I don't know what to say," she said. "You're telling me that I was one of these children? That my mother knew I was some kind of lab experiment?"

It sounded harsh, but she was right.

I nodded.

"And you think I'm in danger?"

"I think if your name is on the master list, then it's possible they're not done with you."

"But you don't know?"

"No," I said. "I don't know."

"Christ." Abby sat up, shook her head. "I need a drink. Do you want one?"

I started to say no, but she stopped me.

"Never mind, I'm making you one." She stood up. "I'm not drinking alone. Not tonight."

"A small one," I said. "We can't stay here for long."

Abby headed for the kitchen.

I stayed on the couch and stared up at the black and red Rothko painting and tried to figure out what we should do next. If what I suspected was true, our best chance was to leave town and not look back. But we'd have to hurry.

Abby came back a few minutes later with two glasses. She handed one to me and sat down, silent.

I took a long drink, then leaned forward, elbows on knees, and said, "Can I ask you something?"

"Why not?"

"You've been sick before, right?"

Abby laughed. "Are you serious?"

"It sounds stupid, I know, but—"

"Of course I've been sick," she said. "Everyone gets sick. I've had colds."

"Did you see a doctor?"

"For a cold?"

"Have you ever been hospitalized?"

Abby frowned. "A lot of people never get seriously sick when they're young. That doesn't mean anything."

"But there's no record of you—"

"No record?"

I stopped talking.

"Forget it," I said. "It's nothing."

"What do you mean there's no record?"

I took another drink. "Your medical records are—"

"How would you know that?"

I could feel her staring at me, wanting the truth. I had to tell her, and I didn't see any way out of it.

"I ran a background check on you before I came out here that first night."

"You what?"

"All I had was your name and this address." I turned to face her. "I didn't know anything about you, so—"

"So you invaded my privacy?"

I nodded. "I guess I did."

"Jesus, Nick." Abby stood up and held out her hand for my drink. "Are you done?"

I drained the last of the scotch, then handed her the empty glass. "Do you want me to leave?"

She seemed to think about the question, then shook her head. "No, but I want you to tell me everything you found out, and I want you to be honest. Can you do that?"

I told her I could.

She stared at me for a moment, then turned and headed for the kitchen. "What proof do you have that I was part of this project?"

"No proof," I said. "Just a feeling."

"So you don't know for sure?"

"Not for sure, no." I pushed myself up off the couch and crossed the room toward the painting. "But your medical records were empty. No illnesses, no doctor's visits, there was nothing. After everything I'd learned about Project Aeon, it seemed to click."

"You mean after what Patricia told you."

"You think she made it all up?"

"Oh no," Abby said. "She didn't make anything up, but as usual she was selective about what she told you."

I listened to Abby moving around in the kitchen, and I stared at the painting. Then I leaned in and reread the handwritten note mounted on the wall.

An original for the original.
With joy,
Daniel

This time something about the note didn't seem right. I read it over again, feeling it gnaw at me, but I couldn't quite place it. There was a warm alcohol buzz building in the center of my chest, and my head felt light and open.

I decided I'd had enough to drink.

"If you're making another, don't make one for me."

"Too late."

I turned away from the painting and saw Abby standing a few feet behind me. It startled me, and I jumped.

"Did I scare you?"

I tried to play it off, but my heart was racing, and I couldn't seem to find the words.

Abby was carrying two drinks.

"I already made these, so you can't back out yet." She held one out to me. "Besides, there are a few things I'd like to know."

I could feel beads of sweat forming on my skin, and the floor seemed to move under me. I reached for the drink and spilled half of it on the back of my hand.

I started to apologize, but then Abby reached out and grabbed my arm, steadying me.

"Let's sit down," she said. "Try to think this through."

Abby led me over to the couch. I struck my shin on the coffee table, spilling more of my drink.

"Damn it," I said. "I'm sorry I—"

I felt the strength run out of my legs, and I reached out and grabbed the arm of the couch, dropping backward onto the cushions. The glass I was holding slipped out of my hand, and I watched it fall slowly, striking the hardwood floor and shattering.

"It's okay," Abby said. "Just be still."

I tried to sit up, tried to apologize, but the room tumbled around me, and I couldn't find my voice. Abby eased down onto the couch beside me.

"Relax, Nick."

Her voice sounded far away, and when I looked up at her my vision blurred, as if seeing her from underwater.

"What the hell is—?"

"All you had to do was walk away," she said. "It was over, and no one would've bothered you."

I followed the sound of her voice, tried to focus. "What did you—?"

"Victor told me you'd come back, but I didn't believe him." She slid out to the edge of the cushion, her legs crossed at the ankles, her hands folded properly in her lap. "Looks like I was wrong."

I reached for the arm of the couch. It took all my strength to pull myself up to a sitting position. Once I did, I looked down at the floor and the broken glass scattered like ice in the spreading pool of scotch.

Abby watched me, her face stony.

"You shouldn't fight it, Nick. You're going to need all your strength."

I tried to stand, but my legs were numb, and I slipped down to the floor, my back against the front of the couch.

"Careful," Abby said. "Don't cut yourself."

I looked down at the broken glass around me, then reached out and picked up one of the bigger pieces and squeezed it hard. The pain was sharp. I felt the edge dig into my palm and the blood run over my hand.

"What did you give me?"

"A little Rohypnol," Abby said. "At least I think it was a little. All of this is new to me."

"Why?"

Abby got up and knelt in front of me. She watched me for a moment, then reached out and touched my cheek with her fingertips, moving them over my skin, gentle and slow.

"Because you came back."

31

For a while I was alone. Then Abby was there, carrying a dustpan and a towel. She knelt on the floor and began picking up shards of broken glass and placing them in the dustpan.

"I bet I can guess what Patricia told you," she said. "She told you my mother started that fire because she was heartbroken over Daniel, and that she couldn't stand the thought of not having him in her life. Am I right?"

She looked at me, smiled.

"You don't have to answer," she said. "I know I'm right, because that was what she told me. Patricia doesn't understand how any woman could look at Daniel and not fall under his spell." Abby shook her head. "She's deranged."

I tried to say something, but the words came out jumbled and loose.

"I'm not saying my mother didn't love him," she said. "How could she not? They worked together, and they shared the same passion right up until the end, when Daniel decided to throw everything away."

Abby picked up the last of the broken glass, then reached for the towel and spread it over the floor.

"They both believed in evolution through science." She sat back on her heels, looked up at me. "Patricia thought it was a cult. I bet she told you that, too, didn't she?"

I shook my head and felt it roll on my neck.

Abby made a dismissive sound. "I'd be surprised if she didn't. That's one of her favorite ways to dismiss Daniel's work. It's no secret she lacks the intelligence and the imagination to understand what they were trying to do. It's easy to tear down the things you don't understand."

I bit the insides of my cheeks hard enough to make my eyes water. It pulled me back.

"You were the first."

Abby's eyes went wide. "Very good, Nick." She nodded. "My parents had boundless faith in their work and in each other. It seemed like the logical place to start testing."

"The original."

Abby smiled. "You mean the painting." She turned toward the Rothko then back to me. "The note was Daniel's attempt at being clever and making me feel welcome. It didn't work on either level."

She looked down at the dustpan, moving the broken pieces of glass around with her finger.

"He had so much guilt when I met him." Her voice was distant. "I was glad, too. It would've been a shame if the years had dimmed his memory of what they did to us."

Abby looked at me, her eyes sharp.

"Now he's dying, a shell of the man he once was and sur- rounded by parasites who only see his money." She shook her head. "Alone and haunted by the memory of his daughters."

I looked up at her.

"Patricia didn't tell you that part, did she?" She smiled. "It's true. Everyone born into that program, we're all his children."

I tried to focus on what she was saying, but my mind drifted, and I closed my eyes. I don't know how long I was out, but when I opened my eyes again Abby was in front of me, slapping my face, bringing me back.

"There you are," she said. "Try to stay awake, okay? I had to guess the dosage, and I'd hate for you to drift off and not wake up."

She patted my leg, then went back to cleaning the spilled drink off the floor. A second later I heard her hiss through her teeth, and she reached for my hand.

"You're bleeding."

I tried to pull away, but everything seemed to be going in slow motion, and all I could manage was a weak twitch.

"Come on, let me see."

Abby pried my fingers open, said, "Why would you do this? I told you to be careful." She stood and disappeared down the hallway. When she came back she was carrying a bottle of rubbing alcohol, a roll of medical tape, and some gauze. "Let's clean you up before everyone gets here."

I made a sound, but she ignored me.

"There's still a lot to do," she said. "We were stuck for a long time, but then you stepped in and saved the day." She paused. "Which makes what has to happen next so upsetting."

I tried to pull my hand away, but she held tight.

"You're going to have to be still if you want me to clean this cut. It's a nasty one, so if I were you—"

"What are you going to do?"

This time my voice sounded clear, and Abby sat back.

"Maybe I didn't give you as much as I thought," she said. "Lucky for you. I was starting to worry."

"Why did—?"

Abby reached for the towel. She slid it under my hand, then opened the bottle of rubbing alcohol and poured it over the cut on my palm. I felt the sting all the way up my arm, but I didn't make a sound.

"Sorry, but it has to stay clean."

I took a deep breath and tried to ask her what they were going to do, but before I could, Abby spoke. This time her voice was low and soft, and I had to strain to hear it.

"I hate the smell of rubbing alcohol," she said. "Always makes me think of doctors, pain, and fear from when I was a child."

I frowned, and she noticed.

"Not the kind of doctors you're thinking of," she said. "These doctors were different. They were terrifying, and they were ruthless."

Abby didn't go on, and I watched her as she wrapped my hand with the gauze. When she finished, she looked up at me and smiled.

"There, good as new." She stared at my hand, but her eyes were still far away. "I don't know how many diseases they infected me with back then, but it seemed like there was a new one every week." She picked up the rubbing alcohol and replaced the lid. "It was painful, but nothing compared to the physical injuries."

For a moment she was gone, lost in thought. When she came back, she looked at me and shrugged.

"None of that matters anymore." She gathered the towel and the dustpan, along with the gauze and the tape. "I was happy when she burned it down."

"Why did she—?"

"Because she loved me," Abby said. "When she saw what they were doing, she tried to get them to stop, but it was beyond her control."

"So she destroyed it."

"She was a scientist, but she couldn't stand by and watch." Abby paused. "I would've done the exact same thing if I were her."

Abby got up and carried everything back toward the hallway. Then she stopped and looked back.

"The good news," she said, "is that now, thanks to you, we can find the people who were responsible, and we can make it right for the ones who weren't as lucky as me."

She smiled at me, then walked away.

I could hear her shuffling around in the bathroom, and I tried to push myself up from off the floor. I managed to get one of my legs under me before falling back down and landing on my side.

A minute later someone knocked.

I heard Abby's footsteps running down the hallway, and I felt a cold rush of air against my face as the door opened and several people stepped inside.

Victor and Ellis came around the corner and into the living room. When they saw me, Victor turned to Abby and said something I couldn't quite hear.

I watched her mouth the word "no."

Victor frowned and turned away.

Abby crossed the room toward me. She stopped halfway and turned to Ellis. "Help me get him on the couch."

Ellis stepped forward, and I felt his hands under my arms, lifting me up and onto the couch. Some of the feeling had come back into my arms, and the room stopped spinning.

Victor came up behind Abby. "What do you want to do with him?"

Abby shook her head, her eyes never leaving mine. "It's not time."

I could tell she was about to say more, but then someone else knocked on the door. Victor turned to Ellis, nodded. Ellis walked down the hallway toward the front door. When he returned, Patricia's driver, Travis, was with him.

Abby ran across the room to him and wrapped her arms around his neck. She pulled him in and they kissed, long and deep. When they broke, I heard her whisper, "Well?"

Travis nodded.

Abby kissed him again, then let go and said, "How?"

Travis spoke softly in her ear. When he finished talking, she turned to me.

"I have the most amazing news," she said. "Turns out that after Patricia left her meeting with you, she went home, took her belt from her closet, and hung herself in her . . ." She looked back at Travis. "Where?"

"Her shower."

Abby nodded. "The police haven't found her body yet, so it hasn't technically been ruled a suicide, but it will be soon. Travis has a true gift with suicides."

I looked up at him, but he didn't see me.

"Now comes the hard part." Abby sat by me on the couch. She folded her hands in her lap, took a long, deep breath, and said, "What to do with you?"

32

L et me go."

Abby laughed. "Would that I could, Nick. Would that I could."

She got up and crossed the room to where Victor was standing. I watched them talk for a while, trying to pick up what they were saying, but my thoughts blended together, then dissolved in my mind like smoke.

I closed my eyes and squeezed my hands into fists. My lips were tingling, and some of the feeling was coming back in my arms and legs. I was still a long way from running, but it was a start.

When I opened my eyes again, there were more people in the house. I didn't recognize them, and they moved from room to room, carrying boxes or furniture down the hall toward the back door.

Abby came back and sat next to me.

She held my hand.

"As you can probably tell, we're leaving," she said. "We still have a lot to do, and the sooner we start, the better. You understand, don't you?"

I watched her, didn't speak.

"And then there's you." Abby sat up, inhaled deeply. "You're such a sweetheart, Nick, but you're also a loose end. We still have such a long way to go, and we can't risk you telling anyone about what we're doing here."

"I don't know what . . ."

My voice cracked, and I coughed.

"We're not going to kill you," she said. "Believe it or not, that's not always the best solution, especially with delicate situations like this. A suspicious murder leads to suspicious cops, and that can be an entirely different kind of problem."

She smoothed my collar with her hand. "We've talked about it, and we believe the best scenario for everyone involved is for you to stay alive."

"What are—?"

Abby put a finger to her lips, shushing me.

"I should probably finish," she said. "One thing I've learned is that when you don't want people to figure out the truth about something, all you need to do is make the truth sound insane."

I watched her, waited.

"Think of it this way," she said. "Let's say the police respond to a call of shots fired at your wife's house. They arrive, and they find her lying on the floor with two bullet wounds in her head. Then they find your gun with your prints on it lying on the floor a few feet away."

I tried to sit up, but she held up a hand.

"Hear me out, Nick," she said. "It's important to me that you understand what's about to happen and that you know it isn't personal."

I stared at her, and all I wanted to do was wrap my hands around her throat and squeeze until she stopped talking, but I couldn't. Every move I made was an effort, and I knew that if I was going to get out of this, I had to save my strength.

I eased back and did my best to stay calm.

Abby nodded. "Thank you, Nick." She sat up and turned toward me. "Once they have a body and a murder weapon, the police will start an investigation. They'll find your fingerprints on the fake rock in the backyard and on the hidden key inside. And then they'll find you a few blocks away, lost in your current state, and covered in your wife's blood."

I bit down hard, but I didn't say a word.

Abby reached up and ran her fingertips under her eyes, wiping away tears. "I am sorry about this. It's been such a difficult decision to make, and it just breaks my heart, but I don't have a choice. Until we purify those involved with my father's work, and until the other girls . . ." She paused. "Until my sisters are safe and accounted for, you're a threat to us."

I kept staring at her, my breath heavy and loud.

"This way, when they arrest you it won't matter if you talk. You can tell them your story about genetically enhanced children created in a laboratory by a dying mad scientist, but . . ."

She stopped talking. Her eyes filled with pity. "All they'll see is a lonely estranged husband whose wife is pregnant with another man's child."

I turned away.

"They'll have her body, and when they match the bullets that killed her to your gun they'll be more than satisfied."

I wanted to say something, but when I tried, all that came out was an empty sound deep in the back of my throat.

"You don't argue the message, Nick." Abby put her hand on my knee. "You just make the messenger sound insane. Turn the message into a conspiracy and then dismiss it."

I looked up at her. "Don't."

She smiled through tears, then leaned close and pressed her lips against my forehead. She held the kiss for a long time before pulling away.

"It'll be okay," she said. "I know this is hard, but try to understand. Your sacrifice is for the greater good."

———

Ellis put an arm under mine and walked me out of the house. Travis followed. When we got to the SUV, Ellis opened the passenger door and pushed me inside.

My head was still clouded, and my muscles were weak, but I could sit up without falling over, and some of the feeling was coming back in my legs and hands.

Small steps.

Travis shut the passenger door, then climbed into the backseat as Ellis walked around to the driver's side. I leaned against the door and looked out the window toward Abby's house. She was standing on the porch with Victor behind her, and all I could see was her silhouette in the doorway.

I thought about the photo of her in the yellow dress and of how out of place it seemed to me now.

Ellis got in and started the engine.

We pulled away, leaving everything behind.

———

I kept my eyes closed as we drove, and I tried to focus on what was happening. Ellis and Travis didn't speak, and the only sounds were the hum of the engine and the low buzz of the highway passing under the tires.

I heard a click from the backseat, and I turned around. Travis had my gun in his lap. I watched him pull the magazine, check it, and then slide it back in.

He never looked at me.

I turned back and stared out at the dark highway and the white line flashing past. I had to figure a way out of this, but I didn't know what I could do. I had some strength in my arms, but that didn't mean anything. It was still two against one, and those were bad odds even on a good day.

I glanced over at Ellis. He had his elbow propped up on the door and his other hand holding the steering wheel at the bottom, calm and relaxed. Outside his window a line of trees blurred past, shadows against shadows.

Then it all came clear.

I looked back at Travis. This time he stared at me. I closed my eyes and let my head roll loose on my neck. I didn't know if it fooled him or not, but it was worth a try.

"How much farther?" he asked. "I don't know if this guy is going to last much longer."

Ellis looked over at me, then up at the rearview mirror. "We've got a few miles. If he passes out, he passes out. It doesn't matter if he's—"

I moved as fast as I could, reaching over and grabbing the steering wheel.

"Hey!"

I felt Travis's hands on my shoulder, pulling me away, but it was too late. I had a good grip, and I pushed the wheel hard to the left, putting all of my weight into it.

The SUV turned sharp, cutting across the highway and slamming into the center guardrail. The sound of tearing metal screamed around us, and when Ellis tried to compensate, I felt the SUV tip up onto two wheels.

Behind me, Travis said, "Oh fuck!"

I felt a cold rush of air on my skin as the SUV lifted up off the road and spun, untethered and silent.

An instant later the world exploded.

33

At first there was only darkness.

Then pain.

I could hear sirens in the distance, and then I was gone again. I came back to a bright light in my eyes, and when I tried to turn away I couldn't move. There was something around my arms and legs. I lifted my head to see, and several hands reached in and held me down.

A woman's voice said, "I need you to be still. You've been in an accident, and it's important that you don't move. Can you understand me?"

"What . . . ?"

I looked around and saw metal walls and black windows. There were rows of small plastic bins, shelves of blankets, and lines of bandages.

"Where am I?"

"You're in an ambulance," the woman said. "You've been in an accident, but you're going to be okay. Can you tell us what you took?"

"The hospital?"

"Try and relax, sir. Do you know what you—?"

"Where are they?" I asked. "The others."

The woman leaned in closer. "Was there someone else in the vehicle with you?"

Again I tried to sit up. "Where did they—?"

The woman pushed me back, and I fought against her. Then I heard another voice say, "He's going into shock."

A man with heavy arms leaned above me and slipped an oxygen mask over my face. I tried to jerk my head away, but every move sent waves of agony up my spine, and I screamed. A second later I felt a sharp pain in my arm and then an easy cold spread through me.

I stopped fighting.

"Try to relax," the paramedic said. "You're going to be fine."

I looked up at her face, deep lines drawn around baby-blue eyes, and listened to the slow whine of the siren. I focused on the pain, letting it remind me that I was still alive and that there was still a chance.

Then the shadows came in like an oil spill, seeping in from the edges of my vision, covering everything, until there was only darkness.

———

I open my eyes to a solid white room.

No windows. No doors.

And I'm not alone.

There are others, watching me, white and faceless. They circle the bed like pale shadows, blending into the walls and the floor and the sky.

Then I see her.

She's standing at the edge of the room, hunched forward, her hands at her sides, staring at me. Once I see her, I can't look away.

"You."

At the sound of my voice, the movement around me stops, and the white figures turn, forming a still circle around my bed.

"Where's Kara?"

I look up at their faces, white sheets, clean and featureless.

"Where is she?" My voice is loud. "Tell me!"

The figures don't move.

I look down at my legs, covered in a thin hospital gown, and I try to sit up.

Then the clicking starts.

The sound is loud, and it comes from everywhere.

The figures step forward, closing the circle. When I look up at them, their eyes open, black and depthless.

The clicking grows louder, like the marching of soldiers or the rattle of insect wings.

The circle tightens around me.

"No!"

I look past them toward her, but she's gone, faded into the white.

"Wait!" I scream. "Where is—?"

I feel hands on me, holding me down.

"No one will know! I won't say any—"

The clicking is louder now, deafening, and my voice is lost in the roar. Their hands press, cold and heavy, and the more I fight them, the harder they push, until all I can do is scream.

I scream until they listen.

I scream until they let me go.

I scream until my throat rips.

"Nick."

I felt a hand on my face—heavy, familiar—and when I opened my eyes, the first face I saw was his.

"Dad."

"Be still," Charlie said. "I'll go find the doctor."

He got up and walked toward the door. I called after him, wanting to know about Kara, but my throat was raw and dry, and all that came out was a low whisper. There was a plastic cup of water on the table next to my bed. I reached for it, but my hand stopped halfway.

I was handcuffed to the bedrail.

I eased back on the bed and looked around. There was an IV attached to my arm and a heart monitor beeping beside my head. I listened to the sound for a moment, then closed my eyes and tried to remember what'd happened. I must've drifted off, because when I opened my eyes again Charlie was back, and he wasn't alone.

"Nick," he said. "The doctor is here."

I looked past him and saw a woman in a white coat and blue scrubs reading my chart. She had silver hair pulled back into a bun, and there were two younger doctors standing with her, both dressed in blue. Behind them a uniformed cop stood in the doorway, watching.

"Where's Kara? Why am I handcuffed?"

Charlie looked back toward the cop, then down at me. "Kara's fine," he said. "Now let the doctor look at you. We'll talk later."

Charlie's eyes were heavy and tired, and I wondered how long it'd been since he'd slept.

"Can I have a drink?" I asked.

Charlie reached for the cup of water. He held the straw while I drank, then said, "Kara was here. She stepped out to grab us dinner, but she'll be back."

"She's not safe," I said. "They're going to . . ."

I looked up and saw the doctor staring at me, and I stopped talking. I turned back to Charlie.

"How long have I been here?"

Before he could answer, the doctor said, "How are you feeling, Mr. White?"

I took a quick inventory.

My chest ached, and it felt like someone had drilled a spike into my head, but otherwise I didn't feel too bad. I told this to the doctor, who nodded, replaced the chart at the foot of the bed, and then took a penlight from her pocket. She checked my eyes, listened to my chest, and then opened my chart again and began writing inside.

"How much do you remember?" she asked.

"I remember the accident," I said. "After that, just flashes. There was an ambulance."

"That's right, good." The doctor closed the chart, handed it to one of the younger doctors behind her. "You suffered a fairly significant concussion, along with three fractured ribs. You'll be sore once the painkillers wear off, but there shouldn't be any lasting damage."

"How long have I been here?"

"You were admitted two days ago," the doctor said. "You've been unconscious since you arrived."

I didn't say anything.

"I don't want you to worry," the doctor said. "You're in good hands. You'll be out of here soon."

"When can I leave?"

"I'd like to keep you here one more night, just to be safe." She smiled at me, patted my arm. "But I don't see any reason why we can't release you in the morning."

I thanked her, then leaned back on the bed.

"Get some rest," the doctor said. "I'll be back in a little while to check in on you."

She walked out of the room, the younger doctors following behind her like little blue ducklings.

I turned to Charlie and held up my wrist. "Why am I handcuffed?"

He shook his head.

I looked past him toward the cop standing in the doorway, and yelled, "Hey, why am I handcuffed?"

"Nick, stop." Charlie put a hand on my arm. "He's only here to watch the door. The detective is on the way. He'll explain everything."

I held up my arm again, rattled the cuff.

"Do you know what this is about?"

Charlie looked at the cop and then turned back to me. "They said you were driving drunk and that drugs were involved. I told them you didn't take drugs, but—"

"I wasn't driving."

Charlie stopped. "They told us you were the only one in the car."

"They're wrong. Abby had . . ."

I tried to sit up, but the pain in my ribs screamed across my chest, and I didn't try again.

"Try to be still, Nick." Charlie moved closer. "You're lucky to be alive. The car you were in was totaled."

I waited for the pain to pass.

Once it did I said, "There were two others with me."

Charlie frowned, said, "Maybe it's better if you keep that to yourself."

"What? No, they have to—"

"You're awake."

I stopped talking and turned toward the sound. Kara was standing in the doorway. She was carrying a white plastic bag weighed down with Chinese food boxes.

For a second I almost thought I saw her smile.

34

I ran through everything that'd happened, and Charlie and Kara listened. When I finished, no one said anything for a long time.

Charlie was the first to speak.

"The other two. Who were they?"

"Ellis was driving," I said. "Travis was in the backseat. I don't know his last name."

"They work for Victor?"

"Ellis does," I said. "Travis was Patricia Holloway's driver. He was the one who started all of this."

"He started it?" Charlie said. "How?"

"He had connections," I said. "Patricia had him find someone willing to take the job."

"Killing the girl?"

I nodded. "But Patricia didn't know that they were . . ." I paused. "Involved."

"He warned Abby?"

"She decided to turn it around on Patricia and use her to get what she wanted."

"And she wanted the names of the people who worked with Daniel Holloway on his project."

"Not just the people who worked on the project," I said. "She wanted the names of everyone involved, and Travis acted as a bridge between Patricia and Victor."

"And Victor is—"

"Loyal to Abby," I said. "That's all I know."

Charlie was quiet.

I glanced over at Kara. She was standing at the window, arms crossed, the afternoon sunlight on her skin.

"Are you okay?" I asked.

She turned to face me, nodded, silent.

Charlie said, "So Travis went back to Patricia and told her what they wanted in exchange for killing Abby. She agreed, but when she went to meet Victor for the first time, she saw you and assumed—"

"That I was Victor." I nodded. "She was a little drunk."

"That was when her plan went off the rails."

"Right up until Abby and I came looking for her."

Charlie sat back, his eyes never leaving mine.

"You're lucky they didn't just kill you and take the flash drive and the money. That would've been easier."

"Suspicious murders lead to suspicious cops."

Charlie frowned.

"Abby told me that the last time I saw her," I said. "It's the reason they didn't kill me outright."

"They could've dumped your body in the woods."

"Could've," I said. "But they need to stay invisible, and leaving a trail of bodies is a risk."

"I don't understand any of this," Kara said, turning away from the window. "If they weren't going to kill you, where were they taking you before the accident?"

I looked away. I'd never mentioned Abby's plan to kill Kara and frame me for the murder, and I wasn't going to mention it now. Kara was starting a new life, and the last thing I wanted was to scare her and make her feel like she wasn't safe.

"I don't know," I said. "I didn't want to find out."

"This experiment," Charlie said. "These girls. Abby was part of it?"

"She was the first one," I said. "There were others, but I have no idea how many are still out there."

"But Abby does?"

"She has the list," I said. "If she didn't know before, she does now."

Charlie seemed to think about this for a moment, then said, "What do you think she's going to do? Are these girls in danger?"

"I think she's trying to protect them," I said. "She called them her sisters."

"Because they were part of the same program?"

"There's more to it than that," I said. "Each of the embryos was cultivated in a lab using Daniel's sperm, so genetically they're all sisters."

"That's horrible," Kara said. "Who were these women? Why would they agree to something like this?"

"Because of what Daniel was promising," I said. "These weren't just healthy children. These were children who were immune to disease, who'd never get sick. To hear Abby talk about it, everyone involved believed they were going to change the world."

Kara put a hand on her stomach, turned away. "I can't imagine."

"I don't have all the answers," I said. "Maybe the police will know more after they find her."

"About that." Charlie cleared his throat. "I don't think telling this story to the police is the best idea."

I looked over at him. "Why am I not surprised?"

"How do you think they'll react to all of this?"

"I don't care."

"You should."

I tried to sit up, winced. "I'm going to tell them the truth, and if they think I'm crazy—"

"You can count on that."

"Then so be it." I kept my eyes locked on Charlie and tried not to react to the pain shooting through my chest. "I'm not going to lie anymore."

Charlie stared at me. "It's a mistake."

"We'll see." I looked toward the cop standing in the doorway, then turned back to Charlie. "When is the detective supposed to be here?"

Charlie didn't answer, so I asked Kara.

She frowned. "Any time now."

———

The detective stood at the foot of the bed with his notebook open. He had a yellow pencil stub in his hand, and he tapped it against the page as he spoke.

"You're saying there were others in the car?"

"Two others," I said. "Travis in back, and a man named Ellis in the front. He was driving."

"Ellis?"

"Mr. Ellis." I pointed to his notebook. "That's how Victor introduced him to me."

"And Victor is?"

"His boss."

I saw him glance over at Charlie, then back to me.

"I'm not making this up," I said. "They were there."

The detective looked down at his notebook. "How much did you drink before the accident?"

"I don't know," I said. "A little, but—"

"Your blood alcohol was point one five," he said. "I'd say that's more than 'a little.' You certainly had no business being behind the wheel."

"I told you," I said. "I was in the passenger seat."

I could hear the tension in my voice, and I reminded myself to stay calm, but it was a struggle.

"You were the only one in the vehicle when first responders arrived," the detective said. "Are you saying the other two just got up and walked away?"

"It's possible."

"There was also a handgun found in the vehicle. It was registered to you." He looked up at me. "Any ideas?"

"Yeah," I said. "They stole it."

The detective frowned, flipped a page in his notebook. "We spoke to the young woman who owned the car. She claimed that you two were friends and that you borrowed the vehicle with her permission."

"Abby."

"Abigail Pierce," he said. "She told us that you've been acting erratically lately. Drinking, drugs."

"That's not true."

"She said you've been distraught over a breakup with your wife, and that she's been encouraging you to leave town for a while to clear your head. She's worried about your state of mind."

I heard Kara inhale, sharp, then whisper, "Oh God."

"Abby is the one behind all of this," I said. "She's the one who—"

The detective turned to Kara. "Did you two split up recently?"

"A year ago," Kara said. "But recently—"

"That has nothing to do with what happened," I said. "Abby is lying to you, and unless you do something it's going to be too late."

"What's going to be too late?"

"She has a list of doctors' names. She's planning on finding them. She's going to—"

"Come on, Nick." Charlie put a hand on my shoulder and squeezed. Then he looked over at the detective. "He has a concussion from the accident. I don't think—"

"I'm not making this up." This time, keeping my voice down was impossible. "I'm telling you, Abby is behind everything, and if you don't do something—"

"Nick." Charlie's eyes flashed wide, and he spoke slowly. "Calm down."

I looked from him to the detective, then to Kara. She was staring at her hands and absently picking at the corner of her thumbnail. There were tears on her cheeks.

I stopped talking.

Charlie walked around the bed to where the detective was standing, then motioned to the door leading out into the hallway and said, "Can I talk to you for a minute, Tom?"

The detective flipped his notebook shut, then followed Charlie out into the hall.

Once they were gone, I reached out for Kara.

"I'm not crazy, you know."

Kara took my hand and smiled, but it never touched her eyes. "I know."

I wanted to tell her not to worry, but I couldn't.

A minute later Charlie came back into the room alone. He closed the door behind him, then turned on me.

"Either you hit your head harder than we thought, or you're completely out of your mind." He walked over to the chair and began gathering his things. "What the hell were you thinking?"

"I told him the truth," I said. "Which is what I should've done from the start, but I didn't, and now look where I am."

"You're alive."

"That's not what matters."

"It is to me." Charlie coughed, stepped closer. "It's all that matters to me."

I kept quiet, and Charlie reached out and squeezed my arm.

"I love you, Nick." His voice was soft. "But goddamn, son, you need to learn when to walk away."

35

The detective made a phone call from the hallway. When he finished, he opened the door to my room and motioned for Charlie. They talked for a while, and when they came back into the room the detective handed me a citation for operating an unsafe vehicle and unlocked the handcuffs.

I thanked him.

"Thank your old man," he said. "He's the reason you're not going to jail today."

I rubbed my wrist, nodded.

He handed the cuffs to the uniformed cop. "Don't make me regret this."

I told him I wouldn't.

The detective turned to Charlie. "You take care of yourself. If you need anything at all . . ."

Charlie waved him off, shook his hand.

Once the cops were gone, Charlie went over to the chairs and started gathering his things.

"You're leaving?"

He nodded, didn't answer.

"I should go, too," Kara said. "It's late. I need to get home."

I tried to smile, but the idea that she had someone waiting for her touched a hollow spot inside me, and I couldn't pretend to be happy.

Kara must've noticed because she leaned over and kissed my forehead. Before she pulled away, she whispered, "Don't worry, Nick. Everything is going to be okay."

I decided to believe her.

———

The next day I checked out of the hospital. Kara had offered to pick me up and take me home, but I didn't want to see her, so I called a cab from the lobby and waited outside until it arrived.

The day was bright, and the sky was clear and blue.

When the cab finally arrived, I gave the driver the address, then sat back and stared out the window as we drove. I didn't say anything else until we got to Jefferson Park and pulled up outside Abby's house.

"This is it right here."

Charlie's car was parked out front where I'd left it. I paid the driver, then got out and stood on the sidewalk, staring up at the house, as he pulled away.

For a long time I didn't move. There was a soft breeze passing through the trees, and the leaves above me shimmered in the sunlight. I breathed it all in, then started up the path toward the front door.

Halfway there, I knew.

The curtains were open, and when I got to the porch, I stepped up to the window and looked inside. The house was empty, the walls bare. Abby was gone.

I walked back to the car, feeling each step.

———

At first it was hard to sleep.

Part of it was my ribs. Any movement sent sharp, jarring waves of pain through my chest, sucking the air out of my lungs and making it impossible to breathe.

Then there were the noises.

Footsteps in the hallway, a neighbor's voice outside my door, even the hum of the elevator would pull me awake, and I'd lie in bed with my eyes wide and my heart racing, focused on the sounds long after they'd faded away.

I spent those first few sleepless nights sitting in my living room with my door bolted, staring out at the stretch of city lights along the horizon, trying not to think.

On the fourth night, I'd had enough.

I packed a few things, then drove across town to Charlie's house. He knew I was coming to stay, but I still rang the bell before I used my key to open the door.

"It's just me, Pop."

Charlie came around the corner, oxygen tank in tow. He watched as I closed the front door. Then he motioned for me to follow him.

"Come on. I've got something to show you."

I left my bag by the door and followed him into the kitchen. There was a newspaper spread open on the counter. He picked it up, checked it, then tapped his finger on the page and handed it to me.

"Halfway down."

I scanned the page and found the headline I knew he wanted me to see.

RENOWNED GENETICIST'S DEATH RULED A SUICIDE

As I read the article, all I could hear was Abby's voice in the back of my mind, telling me that Travis had a true gift with suicides.

When I finished, I handed the paper back to Charlie. I wasn't sure what to say about it, so I didn't say anything.

Charlie opened one of the drawers and pulled out a pair of scissors. He cut the article out of the paper and said, "So it begins."

"What can we do?" I asked. "Who can we tell?"

Charlie looked at me, his eyes tired. "You know we can't tell anyone. She made sure of that."

"Then what do we do?"

"We watch." He held up the clipping. "And we start a file. We keep our eyes open and wait for her to slip up."

"What if she doesn't?"

Charlie smiled. "Everyone slips up eventually."

———

Over the next few weeks, my father spent hours at the library, combing through national newspapers and searching the Internet for any recent suicides involving scientists. He made calls to old cop friends, who were happy to humor him and his new retirement hobby, and they agreed to update him on any relevant cases that came their way.

They understood. Once a cop, always a cop.

Charlie didn't ask me to help, and I didn't offer. I knew that Abby was long gone, and searching for her by following a trail of suicides was pointless. She'd lived on the run her entire life. She knew how to disappear, and if she didn't want to be found, she wasn't going to be found. To me, it didn't make sense to try.

One time I asked Charlie why he bothered. I told him that Abby was a ghost, and that trying to track her was a waste of energy. When I finished talking, he looked at me, frowned, and said, "Is that why you think I'm doing this?"

I walked away and never mentioned it again.

———

All I wanted to do was drive.

I didn't have anyplace to go, but that didn't matter. The road cleared my head, and the longer I drove, the more my thoughts faded into the highway, leaving me empty.

Lost in the gray.

———

A month after I walked out of the hospital, I told my father that I was leaving.

"Where are you going?"

"Depends," I said. "Does Lonny's offer still stand?"

Charlie took off his glasses and dropped them on the table in front of him.

"You want to go to Mexico?"

"It's as good a place as any."

We were sitting at the kitchen table, and the morning sun was bright outside the window. I could hear the traffic from the highway in the distance and the quiet murmur of the television on the counter.

"Are you sure about this?"

I told him I was.

Charlie watched me, and I could tell he was trying to choose his words carefully.

"You can't run from yourself, Nick."

"I'm not running," I said. "I'm searching."

"For what?"

I shook my head. "I don't know yet."

Charlie's face softened. He reached for his glasses and slipped them back on. "I'll call him and let him know you're on your way."

"Thanks, Pop."

I got up and rinsed my coffee cup in the sink. There was a stray black dog passing outside the kitchen window, and I stood there, watching him until he was gone. Then I headed back to my room to pack.

Charlie stopped me. "Nick?"

I turned around.

"About your search." He leaned forward, elbows on the table. "If you let it, it'll find you."

36

I crossed the border on a Tuesday and made it to Lonny's fishing cabin a day later. I didn't know what to expect when I arrived, and as I followed a white-sand road through a thick overgrowth of trees toward a scattering of one-level fishing cabins, I imagined the worst.

I wasn't far off.

Lonny's cabin was standing, barely. After seasons of storms, the roof had been stripped of shingles, the cement foundation was crumbling, and the paint on the warped walls was weatherworn and peeling away in long strips.

No, not far off at all.

I parked out front and sat in the car, listening to the steady roll of the ocean, smelling the salt in the air, and wondering if coming here had been the right choice. It'd seemed like the right move at the time. And with me gone, there was no reason for Abby to go after Kara.

In a way, me leaving made her untouchable.

At least I hoped so.

I got out of the car and walked around the cabin. Lonny had arranged for new shingles, drywall, and paint to be delivered, and I found everything stacked in back and covered with a blue tarp. I checked that it was all there, then went around to the front door.

I'd stopped in Tucson to meet Lonny and pick up the key to the cabin, along with all the tools I'd need to do the repairs. He'd mentioned that the last storm was a bad one and that there might be damage inside.

I held my breath and turned the key.

There was a large hole in the roof, but the air inside smelled clean—no mold, no rot.

The cabin had three rooms. A main room attached to a long hallway that doubled as a kitchen, a bedroom without a bed, and a small bathroom with a claw-foot tub. I walked through each room, checking for signs of damage, but to my surprise it was dry.

I spent the rest of the day unloading the tools from my car and making a list of everything that needed to be done. It was a long list, and by the time I'd finished, the sun was going down over the water, and a chorus of insects sang to me from the trees.

That night I rolled my sleeping bag out in the living room and stared up at a scatter of stars through the hole in the ceiling. They calmed me, and I let my mind wander.

As usual I thought about Kara.

———

The first thing I did was patch the hole in the roof, but it took me longer than expected. By the time I'd finished, I knew I'd need help to do the rest.

Then I found Teddy.

He was an American, or rather a Texan, and he lived in a Chevy van that he kept parked on the beach. He had graying black hair that he cut close to his skull, and a large tattoo of an even larger woman across his chest.

He called her Rosie.

"Like the song," I said. "Whole lotta—"

"No, dude." He stopped me, and the expression on his face turned dark. "She's nothing like the song."

I didn't say anything else about it. But it was hard to hide my disappointment.

———

The only bar in San Miedo doubled as a post office. It had three wooden tables out front on a patio, white plastic chairs, and a choice of beer, whiskey, or tequila.

At least the beer was cold.

For weeks Teddy and I would work a few hours every morning, then walk into town for lunch. Afterward we'd stop at the post office, order drinks, then sit at one of the wooden tables and watch the people pass by until the air turned cool and the sun sat low and red over the water.

We had nothing but time.

I never told Teddy about Abby or about what'd happened back home, and he never asked. It was one of the things I liked about him. We were where we were, and how we got there didn't matter.

All I knew about Teddy was that he'd been a bricklayer in Dallas, and then one day his wife cleaned out his bank account and ran off with a woman she'd met online.

Teddy took it as a sign.

"Most of the time the universe is quiet," he said. "But sometimes, if you listen carefully, it tells you exactly what it wants you to do."

"The universe told you to come here?"

"That's right." He grinned at me, lifted his drink. "Same as you, brother."

Teddy had life all figured out.

———

There was no phone at the cabin, so Charlie sent letters. They'd arrive at the post office about once a week. I'd pick them up and read them at night when I was alone. Every one was written in his nurse's handwriting.

This didn't surprise me. Charlie didn't like to write, but I didn't care. The writing might've been Penny's, but the words were all his.

Most of the letters were short. He'd update me on his health, which doctors he liked, and which ones he believed were trying to kill him. Sometimes Penny would chime in to say that he was still a shithead but that he was doing great.

Mostly, though, it was Charlie.

I wrote back, wanting to know if he'd heard from Kara and if he knew how she was doing, but he didn't respond for a long time. When his next letter finally arrived, all it said about her was that she was doing well and that she was happy.

It made me smile.

———

It took longer than I'd expected, but eventually Teddy and I finished the repairs on the cabin. As usual we celebrated with drinks at the post office.

That was when he told me he was leaving.

"I'm going to head south," he said. "I've got friends who run a resort in Costa Rica. I thought I might give that life a try for a while."

"The universe is telling you to move on?"

Teddy smiled. "I knew you'd understand."

"You got enough money?"

"I got what you paid me," he said. "I don't need any more than that."

I turned and looked out at the street. Part of me was sad to see Teddy leave. We'd become friends, and I would miss our afternoon conversations, but I also knew that nothing in life was permanent.

I held up my beer. *"Buen viaje."*

Teddy smiled. "You're getting better."

I nodded, took a drink, and then stared out at the road and the slow drip of people walking by.

"It's getting late," Teddy said. "Maybe she's not coming today."

"She's coming," I said. "It's Friday. She always comes by on Friday."

"You know her schedule but you don't know her name."

"Not yet," I said. "But someday."

Teddy laughed. "The eternal optimist."

I turned back to the road, silent.

We stayed there for a while longer, finishing our drinks and talking about Teddy's trip south. He told me about his friends in Costa Rica and all about the resort where he was going to live.

I tried to listen, but my mind kept drifting. All I could think about was the girl who walked by every Friday, the girl who smiled at me as she passed, the girl I couldn't bring myself to talk to.

I was about to give up and head home when I saw her.

She came around the corner, same as always. There was an old woman with her, and the girl held her arm in hers as they crossed the road to the post office.

Toward me.

The girl had soft, dark eyes and black hair that ran straight and stopped just past her shoulders. She had a thick hardbound book in her arm that she cradled against her chest as she walked, and when she got close to our table I smiled at her.

She smiled back.

The old woman noticed and pulled her along.

"Ven, Olivia."

They walked by, disappearing through the door leading into the post office.

Olivia.

Once they were gone, Teddy leaned forward, said, "A little advice, Nick?"

"Yeah, sure."

"Tread lightly. The women down here aren't like American women."

"That's a bad thing?"

Teddy shrugged. "Depends on your expectations. Down here, if you touch, you better be planning to stay."

I looked back at the door.

Her name is Olivia.

I thought about that for a moment, then pushed back from the table and stood up. I took a few bills from my pocket and handed them to Teddy.

"What's this?"

"A bonus," I said. "For your trip south."

Teddy stared at the money, then up at me. "You're going to talk to her, aren't you?"

I smiled.

Teddy laughed and took the money. He held it for a moment, then got up. "It's your life, my friend."

We shook, and I watched him walk away.

I knew it was the last time I'd see him, and for a moment I was struck by the loneliness of it all.

Then I thought of her.

Olivia.

I wasn't sure if she'd talk to me, or if I stood any chance of knowing her, but right then it didn't matter. It was enough to know that there was still a part of me willing to try, still a part of me willing to hope.

I turned away from the road and walked through the door and into the post office, my heart beating strong in my chest, the universe whispering poetry in my ear.

ACKNOWLEDGMENTS

I'd like to thank Alan Guthrie, Alison Dasho, and Jacque Ben-Zekry for editing this book. Thank you to Gracie Doyle, Alan Turkus, Daphne Durham, Mikyla Bruder, Jeff Belle, and the rest of the Thomas & Mercer team for bringing it to the world. And thank you to Kurt Dinan, Christina Frans, Ron Earl Phillips, and Mike McCrary for their time and input during the early drafts. Most of all, I want to thank my wife, Amy, for making all of this possible . . . Words, words, words.

ABOUT THE AUTHOR

John Rector is the bestselling author of *The Grove*, *The Cold Kiss*, *Already Gone*, and *Out of the Black*. His short fiction has appeared in numerous magazines and has won several awards, including the International Thriller Award for his novella, *Lost Things*.

He lives in Omaha, Nebraska.